FEAR BY INSTALMENTS

Mike Merriman's big band and his vocalist, Ingrid Lee, are extremely successful. However, returning from touring America, they are questioned by reporters concerning their relationship. Worse still, when Mike's wife disappears, Ingrid is subjected to a campaign of vengeance. The threats and attacks grow in savagery. At home or on stage, Ingrid suffers potentially murderous persecution. Meanwhile, Mike can only strive to put an end to the terror building up so remorselessly — the *Fear by Instalments*.

Books by John Burke
in the Linford Mystery Library:

THE GOLDEN HORNS
THE POISON CUPBOARD
THE DARK GATEWAY

JOHN BURKE

◆

FEAR BY INSTALMENTS

Complete and Unabridged

LINFORD
Leicester

First published in Great Britain

First Linford Edition
published 2012

British Library CIP Data

Burke, John Frederick, *1922* –
Fear by instalments. - -
(Linford mystery library)
1. Suspense fiction.
2. Large type books.
I. Title II. Series
823.9'14–dc23

ISBN 978–1–4448–1040–0

Published by
F. A. Thorpe (Publishing)
Anstey, Leicestershire

Set by Words & Graphics Ltd.
Anstey, Leicestershire
Printed and bound in Great Britain by
T. J. International Ltd., Padstow, Cornwall

This book is printed on acid-free paper

FOR
HARRY & SANDI

1

There were seven or eight of them waiting for us as we came off the airport. A flash bulb blazed, and Ingrid put one hand up to her eyes.

She was even paler than usual. The last hour over the Atlantic had been pretty bumpy. I tried to hurry her past the reporters, but they closed in expertly. She gave them a faint, remote smile.

'What was it like, singing in the States, Miss Lee?'

'They gave us a wonderful reception over there,' said Ingrid. Her voice was cool and quiet — but it was a voice with the power to dominate millions.

'Any particular song that made a hit? . . . What did you think were the main differences between shows there and here? . . . Did you bring back any new ideas? . . . '

The questions drove between us and separated us. Three of the reporters edged me to one side, while the others clustered around Ingrid.

One of my contingent was from *The Music Box*, the trade weekly. He was interested in music and not in gimmicks. He wasn't just asking questions for the sake of asking: he really wanted to know what memories I had brought back of the American jazz scene, whether I had found the musicians I had used over there better than my English band, whether I thought the cool style was on its way out, and so on. There had been stories of my meeting Count Basie and Duke Ellington. What had we talked about? 'And your own brand of music — sleek music, as everyone calls it now — didn't you get involved in a big television discussion on that?'

I tried to answer and at the same time catch what the others were asking Ingrid. They were pounding away at her. I could just hear the rustle of her answers.

'It looks,' said one of the other men with me, 'as though you're building Ingrid Lee up into the same sort of star as your wife used to be.'

'Not 'used to be',' I said. 'My wife is still a star.'

'Yes, sure. But Ingrid Lee's coming up fast, isn't she?'

'She made a terrific hit in the States,' I said. 'Terrific. And we've got some new numbers for her that'll go on to the Hit Parade and stay there.'

'You're shaping her up as the same sort of singer?' he persisted. 'Same hair style, same sort of number. Cool and sleek — the new Sex Chill, is that it?'

'Miss Lee is just herself,' I said. 'That's good enough for anyone.'

Faintly, whisperingly, I heard Ingrid say to one of them: 'No, no truth in it at all. We're just good friends.'

I said: 'Sorry, boys. We're tired. We really must move.'

There was a man in a dark suit and a peaked cap waiting for us. 'Mr. Merriman? Mr. Simons ordered the car as you requested.' It was, as one would have expected from Lew, a very large car. Appearances meant a lot to Lew. For a moment I was almost afraid Liza might be waiting in it; that she might have come to meet me at the airport. But of course she would have brought our own car then. And of course she should be at the Tivoli — probably in the middle of a number right now.

As we swung into the long drab road down into London, I reached for Ingrid's hand. It was very cold.

'What did you tell them?' I asked.

'Just that I'd been so thrilled, and I was glad to be home, and I thought the two latest songs I'd got were wonderful, and that you had picked up a really fine little band while we were over there. And . . . '

'And?'

'That we're just good friends.' She laughed faintly. 'It does sound so corny, doesn't it? And so unconvincing.'

'Yes,' I said. 'It certainly doesn't convince *me*.'

I turned to look at her. Her eyes were dark and forlorn in the shadowed interior of the car, with street lights and an occasional neon sign splashing across her face.

Things were going to be so unpleasant for a while: so awkward and unpleasant.

4

There would be the inevitable publicity; and there would be Liza.

I wasn't looking forward to telling Liza.

I dropped Ingrid at her flat. I stayed with her for five minutes. She didn't say a word until I was leaving, and then she put her fingers on my arm and said: 'Why not leave it a day or two, Mike? Don't rush it. You're tired. She'll talk you out of it.'

'That she won't do,' I said.

'Leave it a little while.'

'I'd sooner have it out right away.'

'All right,' she said. 'You know best.'

It was not just tiredness that kept her so still, so unflurried. She had a gift of repose: I felt that I was drawing strength from her assured calm.

I said: 'There's nothing to worry about.'

'There's something about Liza . . . '

'She can't kill us,' I said. 'She's probably got a pretty good idea of the way things are, anyway. It's only a matter of . . . of saying it right out loud.'

But that, I thought as I was being driven home, was the most difficult part of it.

She was not yet back when I let myself into the flat. I poured myself a glass of brandy and sat in my chair close to the radiogram. After a couple of minutes I reached out and idly lifted the lid. There was a record still on the turntable. Liza simply never took a record off and put it away when she had finished playing it.

I looked at the label. It was one of our own — one of the very first. It had been fun when we did it, and it had become our first big success.

So she had been playing it. I felt a twitch of unease. It wasn't like Liza to get nostalgic. Maybe she had just picked it out at random. Or maybe she had left it there deliberately, ostentatiously, as a sort of reproach in advance for the things she suspected I would have to tell her when I got home.

This was silly. I was getting too involved.

I switched on, and flicked the starter. The stylus descended on the groove, and out came the familiar introduction, the first chorus that had taken so long to work out, and then Liza's chill, fascinating voice.

6

We had come a long way since then.

I heard the click of the door in the middle of a chorus, and reached for the automatic stop. The music slurred into silence as Liza came in. She glanced at the radiogram, and pursed her lips.

She said: 'A good trip, darling?'

Her voice was too hard. I had listened to it hardening recently and losing the soft, insidious note that had made her name.

I kissed her.

'It's good to be back,' I said. It was the sort of thing you simply had to say.

Dispassionately I could see that she was beautiful. That slimness that was nearly a fashion model's gauntness; the set of her head with its burnished black hair throwing up and out the pallor of her face; the half-ironical, pouting lower lip . . . all of it heart-catching once, and now all of it leaving me unmoved.

She was wearing a black dress I hadn't seen before. It suited her. It was like one that Ingrid had bought in New York. That had suited Ingrid, too. But when I looked at my wife now, it wasn't the resemblances that counted: it was the differences. The whiteness of her throat against the black dress was not the whiteness of Ingrid. I couldn't feel any desire for Liza. Not now. Not since Ingrid.

'Any coffee going?' I asked.

Liza went through into the kitchen. In the old days I used to follow her in, and we would talk while we waited. Now I stayed where I was.

'Won't be long,' she said, returning. She slid on to the couch and studied me. Her green-flecked eyes were very wide. 'You look just about done in. A hectic time?'

'Oh, not too bad,' I said.

'Tell me all about it.'

I told her all about it. About the tour, and the broadcasts, and the great alto player I'd found, and the enthusiasm everywhere, and the Symphony Hall concert that had had the audience silent, entranced. And she listened with that remote expression of hers — listened, I felt, not to what I was saying but to something that lay underneath.

At last she said: 'And Ingrid went over all right?'

8

'She's really coming on,' I said.

'Better than I was?'

'It's not the same.' I might still have been talking to the reporter at the airport. I said: 'She's just herself.'

'Oh? I got the impression she was just me all over again. Only younger, of course. And newer.'

'Now, Liza — '

'Say it.' She reached for the cigarette box from the table, and held it out to me. 'Go on, say it. Tell me you love her.'

I took a cigarette. I lit hers and my own. Now I wanted to postpone it. Tomorrow, or the day after, would be soon enough.

She went on watching me.

I said: 'All right. I'm afraid that's how it is.'

'Have you been to bed with her?'

'I'd sooner not — '

'No, I don't imagine you have. If you happen to like icicles, I suppose you can't bear them to melt too soon.'

'That's a silly thing to say.'

'How long do you think it'll take you to get over it?'

The edge on her voice was ragged and ugly. It rasped as it had been rasping on my nerves for quite some time before I went off on the trip.

I said: 'This isn't as cheap as you're trying to make it sound.'

'No?'

'I want to marry Ingrid,' I said.

'I'm sure you do.'

'I'm sorry,' I said.

'Don't apologize.' Her gaze wandered away at last. She glanced around the room as though speculating on what would happen to the fragments of the life we had built up together. 'Maybe you've forgotten,' she said, 'but you're already married.'

'Now, Liza, let's be sensible about this.'

She got up abruptly and went out again to the kitchen. When she came back, she had the coffee cups on a tray. Automatically I reached for the small stool and nudged it into position. It was habit. So many things were habit — kissing Liza good morning, kissing her good night, even making love to her at suitable intervals. I didn't want life to settle down like that. I still wanted there to be moments of beauty and enchantment. Things had gone sour between Liza and me, but that didn't mean that there was no way out, no hope, no gleam anywhere.

'I won't divorce you,' she said suddenly.

She stirred her coffee, and went on stirring it. The spoon tinkled exasperatingly against the edge of the cup.

I said: 'I know it's a bit of a shock right now, but when we talk it over — '

'I won't divorce you,' she repeated. 'Go and live with the woman if you've got to. Get it over with. You'd soon come back.'

'I don't think you understand.'

'No?' At last she let the spoon rattle into the saucer. 'Oh, Mike . . . if I don't understand you, who does?'

'We always agreed,' I reminded her, 'that if anything went wrong, we'd be sensible about it.'

'Quite the young idealists, weren't we? But I'm not like that any longer, my dear.' She leaned forward and drew her lips back in a grimace that made me feel sick: its savagery was too naked. 'I'm a married woman, and I intend to stay that way. I've never wanted any other man but you, and I'm going to hold on to you. No sly little bitch like Ingrid Lee is going to cash in on your sentimentality, my sweet.'

The pain of it got me in the stomach. I sat there holding myself tense, and wished I had waited. I wasn't ready for the viciousness of this now. But I had wanted to get it over with. I hadn't wanted there to be any deceit between us.

Unexpectedly, Liza said: 'But you're tired. You're in no state to talk sense tonight.'

'I wanted you to know right away.'

'Let's postpone the details until tomorrow. You can get it out of your system then. We'll go out somewhere nice after the show, and talk it all over. Sensibly, as you suggest.'

The mockery in her tone was not encouraging.

'Sensibly,' I echoed. All at once I felt that my eyes were going to close. I just wanted to go to sleep.

'But,' said Liza, 'don't make any

mistake about it: there'll be no divorce.'
She finished her coffee, although mine
was still too hot to drink. 'If you want me
out of the way,' she said, 'you'll have to
kill me.'

2

I woke up late the next morning. Liza had gone out. I boiled an egg and made some toast, and then Lew Simons rang.

As agents go, Lew is a good agent. He knows everything that goes on, and when nothing much is happening he sets to work on his own to make it happen. His main trouble has always been a boyish love of hugging big surprises to himself. He goes in for prolonged negotiations without giving a hint of what he is doing, and then presents you with the finished deal. 'Aren't I clever?' says every protuberant bone behind his lean, swarthy face. Nothing hurts him more than a lukewarm reception. You have to go along with Lew — and I must admit that if you do go along with him, you tend to arrive at some pretty prosperous places.

This morning he started off by welcoming me home. I had never known him less than effusive, and on this occasion he was positively ecstatic.

'The reports we've been getting back, Mike, boy! You must have slayed 'em over there.'

'We did pretty well,' I said.

'Pretty well! That's how he puts it! Listen, your price has gone up as from the day we got those first reports. I haven't been sitting around, you know, Mike. You know me.'

'Yes, I know you.'

'I've got something that's going to make you very happy. Quite a deal, this one. If it doesn't make you happy, my name isn't Lew Simons.'

I could have pointed out that his name was, in fact, Leopold Szymbraiowski, but refrained. Perhaps he had managed to forget that.

I said: 'But I'm not in the market for any deals, am I? We're nicely tied up with the Tivoli.'

'Fronting a big band,' said Lew scornfully — Lew, who had once persuaded me that the gold would never start rattling in my pockets until I got myself a large band and a lot of fancy

15

music-desks. 'All those lights, all that show business stuff — you always said how much better it was the other way. Like on your tour, now. How many were there in the American combo?'

'Seven,' I said.

'And you played yourself?'

'You know darned well I did.'

'Enjoy it?'

'Same answer.'

'Look, Mike' — it was almost as though he was breathing hotly in my ear — 'come round and see me. This morning.'

'Shall I bring Ingrid?'

He hesitated. 'No. Let's settle it ourselves first. Then, when we've got it all sewn up — '

'Then we can give her a wonderful surprise,' I finished for him. 'You can watch the stars sparkle in her eyes. The glitter of gratitude. Gee, but you're wonderful, Mr. Simons.'

'All right, all right. Have your fun. But just come round here, that's all.'

When he had rung off I ate my toast and wondered. I didn't wonder very hard:

my private life was more important to me at present, and involved a lot more problems, than did the business of making a living.

I dialled Ingrid's number. When she answered she wiped away a lot of my worries. She sounded so undisturbed. She had the inner tranquillity that made her so desirable — and yet so elusive.

I said: 'Darling. Sleep well?'

'I lay awake for a while.' It was simply a statement of fact, not an appeal for pity. 'How did everything go?'

'I told her.'

'What did she say?'

'She wasn't very happy about it. But we didn't expect her to be, did we?'

'You think she will make difficulties?' I noticed, as I had noticed before, that on the telephone Ingrid's voice had a tinge of something alien, a neatness that was almost foreign. It was something we ought to be able to bring out more when she sang.

I said: 'It'll all be all right.'

'But of course.'

'After tonight's show at the Tivoli,' I

said, 'we're going to go and have dinner somewhere. Some quiet place, where we can talk it over. I imagine she'll want to spend today sorting things out in her mind.'

'Yes.'

'It's going to be all right,' I insisted.

'It is just that there is something about Liza . . . '

'Can I see you today?' I said. 'Let's make it lunch.'

'You have seen me enough lately.'

'Lunch,' I said.

'You give the orders.'

'I'll call for you at twelve-thirty.'

'I will be ready.' And then she said: 'Don't worry too much, will you? Think it all out quietly, so you will be able to deal with Liza this evening.'

I hoped I was going to be able to live up to her placid certainties. I couldn't let her down — not in anything, not in the smallest possible way.

I went out into the grey morning. London cold was different from New York cold: it was danker, less invigorating.

Liza had taken the car, leaving no

18

message. I hailed a cab and went to see Lew Simons.

He kept me waiting for five minutes. I could hear the faint murmur of an argument going on inside his office. When the door opened, a young man with flushed cheeks and a petulant mouth came out. He looked at me crossly, then looked again. He forced a smile.

'Hello, Mike. Congratulations. I hear the tour was a great success.'

'Thanks, Tommy.'

He was a bandleader now, trying to keep a big beat band together on the strength of radio bookings and one-night stands all over the country. Not so long ago he had been a good lead trumpet. It was likely that he would soon be looking for a trumpet chair again. There were too many headaches in running a band. So he was polite to me — just friendly enough, just respectful enough. He might need to come to me.

'Mike, my boy. Come on in. Come right on in.'

Lew folded both his hands over my right hand and pumped it up and down.

He let go only in order to move an already well-placed chair a few inches closer to his desk.

'Sit down, sit down.'

I sat down, and said: 'Come on, now. What's all this vague stuff about a new deal?'

'Let me get my breath, boy.'

He looked relieved when the telephone rang. It would have been against his most cherished principles to get down to the main business right away. The telephone provided a decent interval. When the call was ended he tossed a morning paper across the desk at me. 'Seen that one?'

I was looking at a photograph of myself standing beside the car as Ingrid got in. She had half-turned towards the camera, and the oblique shadow of the car roof had blended strangely with her hair. It left only the beautiful oval of her face, cut out of the surrounding darkness. It was as white as a mask, and oddly childlike without the hair.

'Not a very good picture,' I commented.

'It's publicity, boy. And a nice story

about Ingrid as the Snow Queen. Says that the sound of her singing goes into your heart like a sliver of ice. The picture fits, all right.'

I folded the newspaper and put it back on his desk.

'You didn't bring me here just to show me that.'

He leaned back in his chair and put on what I recognized as his tantalizing expression.

'Don't tell me,' I said, 'you've got me a booking in *Listen with Mother*.'

'Sometimes,' said Lew, 'I don't think you really appreciate me.'

'What am I supposed to appreciate?'

'In the first place,' he said, 'you know you can go back to the States any time you want? I've got three firm offers right here.'

'And *you* know,' I said, 'that I'd never want to work there permanently. 'So . . . in the second place?'

He took a deep breath. 'How would you like to play in the Starglow Room at The Caravel?'

I looked suitably impressed. It didn't

require much of an effort. The Caravel was not just a hotel, it was a palace: a small, expensive, exclusive palace. But once I had looked impressed I had some questions to ask.

'What about the Tivoli contract?'

Lew now switched to his pleased expression — the one he wore when he had contrived something complex and rewarding. He said:

'The Tivoli outfit is essentially a show band. There's a danger of it losing the sort of — well, you know how it is, the distinctive personality of your music. It wouldn't do you any good to be fronting the band there for too long. Not intimate enough.'

'All very true,' I agreed; 'but how do the Tivoli boys look at it?'

'The way I see it is this. You can still be responsible for the provision of an orchestra there, and for the musical arrangements. It can carry your name, as it's been carrying it while you've been away in the States. And it can be fronted by Liza — just as it has been while you've been away.'

'Well,' I said. 'Well . . . '

'I've talked to Graber at the Tivoli,' said Lew happily, 'and he's got no objection. They go for Liza in a big way there, you know, and she's done a grand job.'

'Stepping into my shoes, h'm?'

'For crying out loud,' Lew exploded. 'I thought I'd be doing you a good turn. Getting you a chance to play the kind of music you say you prefer — and for more money. And' — his eyes strayed meaningly to the newspaper on his desk — 'saving you some embarrassment in other directions, maybe.'

'Yes,' I said. 'I see.'

'The Caravel,' he said, 'would like Ingrid as part of the deal. So it seems to me this is better for everyone. Unless I've got everything mixed up in my mind, that is.'

It was no good telling him that he had got everything mixed up in his mind. He knew, all right. And this sounded pretty good. In every way it sounded good.

I said: 'When would I have to start?'

'A month next Saturday. Plenty of time to get a band together and build up a good book. All the sleek arrangements you like — all dead right for the Starglow Room.'

'Yes.'

I thought of myself going home and telling Liza — and then realized that it wasn't going to be that way any more.

'Shall I go ahead with the contract?' said Lew.

'Yes. Go ahead. I suppose I'd better start looking around for some good men.'

Lew nodded happily. 'Start sounding them out.'

Then I remembered something. I said: 'But don't forget we've still got some Sunday evening concerts lined up in the provinces with the full band. I'm committed to appearing on those dates.'

'That's right. You'll have to go through with them. But there are only four or five.'

'Who shall I take — Ingrid or Liza?'

His happiness oozed away. He looked wary. 'That's up to you,' he said. 'I suppose it depends . . . '

'Exactly,' I said.

'Is everything going all right with you?'

he probed. 'I mean — can you manage?'

'I can manage.'

'There won't be any nasty blow-up, will there?'

'None,' I said. I hoped I was right.

'A bit of publicity won't do any harm,' said Lew. 'But we don't want it to get out of hand.'

★ ★ ★

On the way to lunch I bought a copy of the newspaper with the picture of Ingrid and myself. Altered as it was by the camera, I wanted to study her face. It might reveal something of her; it might help to peel away some of the mystery and help me to understand who and what she was, and why I loved her. I was somehow never able to study her when I was with her.

As she had promised, she was ready. Her lips were cool and moist when she kissed me. Her skin had a fresh, tingling scent.

'Where are we going?' she asked.

'The Caravel,' I said.

'So?'

'If we're going to work there,' I said with exaggerated casualness, 'we ought to case the joint first.'

'Work there?'

We went out into the street and I hailed a taxi. As we were driven to The Caravel, I explained. Ingrid smiled her tight, self-possessed little smile. It was impossible to tell whether she did not fully understand the status of The Caravel, or whether she was simply hugging the sense of achievement, of ultimate success, to herself.

Men looked up as we went into the restaurant. So did the women,

When we had ordered, I passed the newspaper across the table to her, folded back at the right page.

'Seen this?'

She took the paper, and looked at the picture. I saw her stiffen. It was the only time I had ever seen her startled.

I said: 'Anything wrong?'

'It is not a very good one,' she said slowly. 'It is not me.'

'Not really,' I agreed; 'but it's quite

striking. I wondered if it was just a facet of your personality I hadn't noticed before.'

She handed the paper back without another word.

I glanced round the room. I had been here often enough before, but now there was a new significance in everything I saw. This was the right atmosphere for my kind of music. Sleek and expensive; subdued in spite of the rattle of knives and forks and the swift servility of the waiters.

It was rather different, I thought suddenly, from the coffee bar in which Ingrid had sung not so long ago. This was where she belonged. And she took it all for granted. I could almost have been angry with her. I could almost have demanded that she admit how lucky she was. I'd had to fight my way up, while she had just walked in at the top.

My drummer, Clyde Goff, had discovered her. He came in to a rehearsal one Monday and told me that he had heard a wonderful impersonation of Liza the previous evening. 'Almost realer than the real thing,' was a phrase he used, I remember. Some girl singing in a coffee bar had been taking off popular vocalists of the day. Her version of Liza's songs had been far and away the best. I really ought to go and hear her. Just for the fun of it, I really ought to listen. And watch. I said 'Oh, yes?' and thought no more about it — impersonations in coffee bars were not likely to draw me out on a Sunday evening — until a fortnight later, when Liza decided to go up to spend the day with her mother in Durham, coming back on a night train. This left me with a day to myself. I spent it lazily — lying in bed with the Sunday papers, listening to the radio, and going out for a late lunch. In the afternoon I sketched out an orchestration, enjoying myself because I didn't have to do it right now and feeling virtuous about the fact that I *wanted* to do it. In the evening I went out for a stroll, had a drink, and found myself guiltily experiencing an unusual feeling of freedom. The routine of running a band was a hard one. The more in demand we got, the harder it got. Success depended on our regular spot at the Tivoli, regular Sunday evening concert appearances, and gramophone recording sessions. There were broadcasts and television appearances. Leisure hours were rare. And Liza . . . Well, Liza was beautiful, she was part of our success, she was my wife, she had come up with me from the rough days to the rich ones — and the excitement wasn't there any more: I knew her too well now, and there was none of the thrill of discovery, of challenge.

I came to myself with a start. This wasn't the sort of thing I wanted to think about Liza. I stared fiercely at some shirts in a window, moved on past a shuttered jeweller's, and found myself outside the coffee bar which Clyde had mentioned.

There were climbing plants just inside the window. Through the twisted stems I could see the usual small tables and angular chairs, the usual gleaming coffee machine and the panels of clashing colour on the walls. A boy with a guitar was perched on a stool at the end of the narrow room. A girl in a blue overall carried two plates from the counter to a table.

I pushed the door open and went in.

The strumming of the guitar was lazy and formless. It provided a background that was mellow and indecisive enough not to drag too insistently at the attention.

The girl came to serve me. She had black hair tied loosely in a ribbon at the back, and her legs were bare. She wore sandals that fell away from her heels as she walked. I ordered a black coffee, and watched the exquisite balance of her body as she walked away.

When she had brought the coffee she looked round. Nobody else had come. There was a buzz of conversation. She went to the guitarist and he grinned. The next few chords he played were much more decisive.

She began to sing.

The first number was up tempo, and she dragged it slightly in the way Billie Holliday might do it. She got the same despairing rasp into her voice, and the same trumpet quality; but it wasn't her sort of song — her face was too calm and remote for it.

All the same, she was good. We all clapped. She lifted her shoulders very slightly, and then cleared some plates away from one of the tables. The guitarist played an interesting, tortuous modulation while he waited for her, then slowly worked his way into some introductory bars that I recognized very well. I watched the girl walking back, lifting her chin and parting her lips, ready to sing.

This time she was Liza. Only more so. Realer than the real thing, as Clyde had put it.

It was an old song. It was the one that had first got Liza dubbed 'the Sex Chill,' and it was from that beginning that we had made her what she was. *You Leave Me Cold* . . . it was a number that had become almost a joke with us nowadays, and when she sang it — as she often had to in answer to requests — it made no impression on me at all. The authentic, disturbing chill wasn't there any more for Liza — or for me.

But this girl had it. Her singing was all that the number demanded: she was indifferent, almost contemptuous. She was all that I had built Liza up to be. Only more so.

I think I must have wanted her from that very first moment.

When she had finished, and two men in the corner were asking her to do another one right away, the older woman who sat at the cash register came bustling along the room. She shot me a frightened glance — a glance of recognition — and went and whispered in the girl's ear.

The dark eyes turned towards me in bland disbelief. I tried to smile: she made me feel that I ought to apologize for being there.

Instead, when she came to my table again, I said: 'Would you be interested in coming to an audition? I'd very much like to fix one for you.'

'Really an audition?' she said.

'Really.'

After that first sardonic expression of doubt, she accepted it all calmly. It was arranged. The thing began; and six months later we were sitting at lunch in The Caravel.

And I still knew very little about her.

I said: 'How are you proposing to spend the afternoon?'

'Having my hair done. And you?'

'I'd better go round to the Tivoli and see how things have been shaping.'

I wanted her. Yet when the time came — when it was all right, and we were together — would I feel as reluctant as I did now to shatter the mystery of her? It was absurd. I wanted to see that flawless mask distorted by passion . . . to see the calmness gone from her eyes; and yet I wanted her never to be other than she was now.

I said: 'Don't you want to know how I got on with Liza?'

'Only when you're ready to tell me, darling.'

After all, there wasn't much to report. 'She said' — I tried to make it sound as ridiculous as it obviously was — 'I'd have to kill her if I wanted to get her out of the way.'

Ingrid went on eating her moussaka. At last she said: 'This isn't going to be easy.'

'It won't be quite as melodramatic as it sounds,' I said. 'We'll be talking it over this evening — rationally. I'll give you a ring tomorrow morning and tell you how it worked out.'

'Yes,' she said. 'Do that.'

★ ★ ★

Later I went round to the Tivoli. The band was running through a couple of new numbers ready for the evening's show. Liza was there. She was singing as I came in. It was a pop that was going to be plugged a lot in the next few months. It didn't seem to me to be Liza's sort of song at all: it was maudlin and nostalgic, and she was making quite a torchy effort out of it. I stood at the far side of the auditorium and waited until she had finished.

My band was a big one, but when the place was empty like this it looked a very small outfit in the middle of that vast space. Echoes throbbed back from the deserted balconies. The serried ranks of tables were desolate; the dance floor was nothing but a smooth sounding-board.

Liza's voice sobbed in the resonant cavern.

The number finished with the muted brass sighing away into nothingness. I went across the floor.

'Hello, boss — welcome home.'

'Brought any five-cent cigars back?'

Liza looked down at me questioningly as I reached the platform.

I said: 'Trying that one out on them tonight?'

'You don't like it?'

'It's a bit sticky,' I said.

'It's nice,' she said. 'It reminds me of some of the tunes we used to like in the old days.'

The old days. I climbed up and stood in front of the band, and thought of the silly things I would probably have done with an outfit this size when I was younger. Then it would have been a matter of pounding out the Goodman-Henderson sort of thing, or even some Bob Crosby arrangements. A hell of a row we'd have made with a sixteen-piece band in those days, let alone the twenty-four that I'd got now — including strings.

I thought of the sextet there was going to be at The Caravel.

'Everything going all right?' I asked Freddie, at the piano.

'We've been churning it out. No fluffs. No complaints from the neighbours.'

'Let's hear that arrangement of *Autumn Haze*. I didn't have a chance before I flew out.' One of the sax section glanced quickly at his watch. 'Then,' I said, 'maybe you'll be packing up until tonight.'

Freddie passed the scribbled score over to me. I propped it up on the end of the piano and beat the band in. They played it well. It sounded better than I had thought it would. It was hazy and unsettled, just the way I had wanted it to be. The sour progressions in the brass worked out beautifully.

When it was over I went to Liza. The boys began shuffling away. They had a few hours before the show began tonight — the continuous dancing, the cabaret, the spinning coloured lights.

I said: 'I'll pick you up after the show.'

'You're not going to take over right away?'

'Saturday evening I'm due back,' I said, 'and Saturday evening it is. You and

Freddie can cope, can't you?'

'Nobody's shot us yet.'

'Where would you like to go tonight?'

'The Chord,' said Liza.

I had expected her to shrug and say that it didn't matter: anywhere, so long as it was quiet and we could talk.

I said: 'But we won't be able to hear ourselves speak.'

'If it's too noisy,' she said, 'you can do some thinking instead.'

'But — '

'I want to go to The Chord,' she insisted.

I wondered what she hoped to achieve. The place was bound to revive memories for both of us. But I was beyond the reach of memories. That was what I must make her realize: she must be made to understand, to accept and be sensible.

3

The Chord club was behind Oxford Street, down a flight of steps. You could hear the thump of the bass drum from some distance away, steadier than the throb of the traffic, and when you got to the top of the steps the faint argument of trumpet, clarinet and trombone drifted up to greet you. It was the same sort of sound that we had made a long time ago, the other side of the war, in just such a smoky room in a basement. I had come a long way since then. Dave Blair hadn't wanted to come all that way. Dave was still content to be below street level.

I pushed the door open and held it open for Liza. The noise swelled up. We walked right into a riding chorus of *Stealin' Apples*.

The ceiling was low, and the smoke clung to it. Candles guttered in old wine bottles on the tables. Three couples were dancing: they were younger than most of the people there. This wasn't a jazz club for teenagers so much as a haunt for those who remembered — those who still talked about Bix, Joe Sullivan, Mildred Bailey, Fats Waller and the early Count Basie, and who got a bit dewy-eyed if you played *Easy Living*.

It had its advantages. You could eat here. You didn't have to stand round sipping Coca-Cola and getting earnest.

We had a table away from the band. Smoke from the wavering candle flame drifted into my eyes. It wasn't a bit like The Caravel.

There was a pause. I ordered, and we got a bottle of wine. It was just that and nothing more: a bottle of red wine. It tasted tart, even vinegary, but Liza smiled reflectively as she lifted her glass.

'To our future,' she said ironically.

I said: 'We might as well get down to — '

The band blasted off suddenly. Heads came up as the customers recognized an oldie. Dave, with his hair untidy — not romantically wild, just untidy — as it had always been, closed his eyes and squeezed the melody out of his trumpet while the rest of them riffed along behind him. They had no fixed style. They played as we had played in those immediately pre-war years — picking up a tune and kicking it casually around. Dave hadn't progressed at all, either forwards or backwards. While the bop and progressive boys had been righteously abandoning key signatures and sixteen-bar sequences in order to express their contempt for the limitations of primitive jazz, and the New Orleans revivalists had been assiduously learning to play out of tune in order to express their contempt for the bop and progressive boys, Dave had gone on playing the way he felt like playing. It sounded dated, yet oddly timeless.

'Takes you back?' said Liza.

'Amazing how Dave has refused to develop,' I said.

'Things were better then,' she said. 'We had such fun.'

Yes, we had certainly had fun. It was all new then. We waited for the rare, infrequent records to get through from America, and sat enraptured over the canned sound of the Goodman Trio, or of an early Louis reissue. Jack Teagarden's croaky trombone broke through here and there, with this recording outfit and that. Voices — the voices of young Ella Fitzgerald, Billie Holiday, Teagarden and Jimmy Rushing — set the pattern of the time, the sound of the time.

But you couldn't stay still. You couldn't allow yourself to stagnate. If you did, you stayed in a cellar like this for ever.

I tried to make it friendly. I said: 'It wasn't fair of you to bring me here. I'll be weeping into the wine any minute.'

The candlelight flickered on her face. It was late, and she looked tired after the long show at the Tivoli. 'I've got the right to use what weapons I can,' she said.

My throat tightened. The discussion had got to start. The longer I waited, the worse it would be. I refilled Liza's glass and my own, and said:

'We didn't come here to listen to the music.'

'I'd be perfectly happy to do so.'

'Liza, I wasn't joking last night.' The band was pounding into a slow blues. I had to lean across the table. 'It's no good pretending that we can make a go of things any longer, is it? We haven't been right together for a long time.'

'Haven't we?'

She was not going to make it easy. For months she had been stiff and hostile, caught up from time to time in bouts of nagging, at other times sunk in a sullen disregard for me, for music or for anything; but now she was trying to act as though outraged by truths which she had never suspected.

I said: 'You've told me yourself that I didn't seem to be with you half the time. Well, now I'm admitting it. We haven't been talking the same language. Why not face it?'

'You find me physically repulsive?'

'For heaven's sake . . . '

'You want to trade me in for a new model,' she said savagely. 'Maybe somebody else can use me for a while before I'm knocked down as scrap.'

Women say just what they want to say, and make it hurt. And when you've got the answers, when you can bring up a thousand examples of their own viciousness, you somehow can't lash out at them. You just try to be reasonable — for all the good it does.

I said: 'Are you happy, Liza? Have you been happy with me — just lately, before I went away?'

'I thought I was happy,' she said, 'a couple of nights before you went away.'

I ought to have expected it. For this one I had no answer. I had made love to her, trying to recapture something and to assure myself it was going to be all right and I wasn't going to tell Ingrid all the things I wanted to tell her; and I had bought Liza some jade earrings she longed for; and that night she had been wonderful; and afterwards I was ashamed.

I said: 'But the rest of the time? Liza, we'll never get anywhere if you're not honest.'

'Where do you *want* to get?' she snapped. 'Into Ingrid's bed? It's not up to me to help you. You needn't expect me to back out politely.'

The band stopped. There was a spattering of applause. We could talk more quietly. But then it was worse: I seemed to be clenching a fist round my words, twisting them tightly out.

'It's not that you want me,' I said. 'It's simply that you can't bear to let anyone else have me. Possessiveness, that's all it is. You know there's nothing left, but you won't let go. We might both of us have a chance of starting again, without smearing the good things we used to have — the way it was with us at first . . . '

'You make me sick.' She put both hands flat on the table. She was crouching as though about to spit at me. 'The way it was with us at first!' she echoed mockingly. 'That's what you're always trying to do, isn't it? Groping for your adolescent enthusiasms. Wanting to be young and ardent again. Perpetual springtime for Mike Merriman! Mad, passionate love — and a brand-new number for the band every night.'

'Liza, you'll cheapen everything. You'll make it impossible — '

'Ah, the careless rapture!' She gave the impression of screaming in an undertone. 'Just because you've known me too well, for too long, I won't *do* any more, will I? And after a year or two, when the ravishing Ingrid turns out to be just a woman like any other, just as dissatisfied and tired of the perennial playboy . . . '

She looked up, and in the blurred light her features seemed to dissolve. They reshaped into a smile.

'Dave, my dear — how are you?'

'Well,' said Dave. 'Well, this is an honour. Slumming?'

He lowered his massive body into a chair. In the background the interlude pianist was playing a Jess Stacy solo. Dave prodded at his plump lips with his forefinger.

I said: 'You're in form tonight, Dave. But then, you always are.'

'Meaning that I play the same old trash over and over again?'

But he wasn't prickly. The remark was lazy and good-humoured. He didn't care: you could tell when you listened to his playing that he had a wonderful creative imagination — but it seemed to stop short somewhere along the line.

Liza said: 'Business good?'

'It's not the Tivoli,' he said, 'but we can't complain. The old faithfuls come rolling along to see that we don't starve. Of course, they're dying off year by year as old age grips them, but there always seems to be an adequate supply of nostalgic prowlers. Like yourselves,' he added, looking straight at me.

I was still keyed up. I didn't want to relax and let the determination drain out of me. This was a time for breaking all the news there was to be broken. And I had an idea. It really appealed to me. Quite apart from that, though, it was a good way of telling Liza.

I said: 'Would you like a good job in a small outfit, Dave?'

Liza stared at me, puzzled.

'One of yours?' said Dave.

'Right with me. I'll be playing in it myself. A smooth sextet — scope for anything we want to do. In the Starglow Room of The Caravel.'

He whistled.

'But what about the Tivoli band?' Liza demanded. 'You're not going to break that up?'

'It stays where it is,' I said, 'with you in command.'

'Oh,' she said. 'Oh. I see.'

Dave said: 'What kind of music will they be wanting at The Caravel?'

'With a bit of perseverance,' I said, 'we can make them like what we like. We can experiment. It's a lovely set-up.'

'You're trying to corrupt me.'

'Look, Dave' — quite apart from any other considerations, I realized that I wanted him very much to be playing alongside me again — 'you can't go on drowsing along like this for ever. Dredging up the old stuff, year after year . . . Damn it, you're nothing but a case of arrested development.'

He grinned. 'It's the way the music comes out,' he said. 'I just let it come out, and to hell with gimmicks.'

'But you're refusing to let yourself work out a distinctive style,' I argued. 'There's nothing creative about this . . . this chorus playing you go in for.'

'Creative? Listen, Mike. Sometimes we feel like playing loud, so we play loud. Sometimes we want it quiet and rocking,

47

so it's quiet. We don't smooth everything out or dress it up. We play it how it comes.'

'I wish you'd give yourself a chance,' I said.

'Mike . . . I'd love to be sitting in with you. Believe me. I still have dreams, sometimes, about the way you used to play piano.'

'I'm going back to it,' I said. 'And I'm offering you a job.'

'The price is too high,' he said firmly.

Before I could argue any further, Liza said: 'If I'm with the Tivoli outfit, I suppose you'll be taking Ingrid into the Starglow Room.' It was a statement, not a question.

'That's the way Lew Simons sees it,' I said. Then, because that sounded cowardly, I quickly added: 'And the way I see it, too.'

There was a silence. At least, that was what it sounded like, although I could still clearly hear the pianist working away on something from the Chicago days.

At last Dave said: 'One woman at the Tivoli, and one in the Starglow Room.

You certainly live it up, don't you, Mike?'

There was a rough edge to his voice. He had always been fond of Liza, and he must have sensed that there was something wrong. And if there was something wrong, of course I got the blame. Not that I gave a damn now. I just wanted it settled. I was glad when the piano stopped and the band reassembled. Dave got up and patted me on the shoulder with a sort of sad affection that made me want to stand up and hit him.

'Don't overdo it, Mike,' he murmured. 'You can't take it with you — or her, or them.' He swung towards Liza. 'Give me a ring one day. I can't afford the Starglow Room, but we might have a bite at a Corner House.'

He went back to the stand. There was a pause. Liza and I did not speak. Then, when the band swung out into *Changes*, I said:

'Sorry we were interrupted. We should have gone straight home after your show.'

'So I'm to be the resident icicle at the Tivoli? Very convenient for everyone. And while I'm being the Sex Chill there, the temperature at The Caravel will get even lower. It's all neat and tidy in your mind, isn't it, Mike?'

I wished it were. I wished I could simply say, outright and without having to wrap it up, that I was weary of her. I'd gone dead on her, and what was the use of arguing about it? I wasn't mad or filled with hatred, or anything: just tired.

'It's over,' I said as bluntly as I could manage. 'Won't you accept that?'

'Mike.' She was leaning forward again. 'This isn't going to be tidied up just like that. Someone's going to get hurt — and it isn't going to be me.'

'Why won't you admit that you're just as fed up as I am with the whole set-up?' I flung the words into her unresponsive face. 'Let's put an end to it. We're civilized intelligent people. I'm tired. You're tired — '

'Tired, yes. Tired of being the Sex Chill. What a beautiful character to have foisted on you! I'm tired of being your invention — so much your invention that even at home you don't like me to be myself. I've nearly forgotten what I am

. . . what I *was* before you dreamed up this idea. Well, Mike, I suppose this is when I start finding out again. You've managed to lose yourself somewhere; but I'm not going to get lost. I'm going to find out what there is buried down inside me — what I'm capable of.'

An ensemble chorus that was too loud for comfort came blasting across the floor. Until it ended we couldn't speak. She stared her accusation at me all the time.

As the last chord echoed away, I said: 'I don't want it to finish like this, Liza. Surely — '

'You're a fool.' A half-forgotten North Country harshness was back in her throat. 'You've got a lot to learn — and, by God, you're going to learn it. You'll thank me one day. Whatever it costs, before I've finished you'll be sorry you ever thought about Ingrid Lee. And when you see for yourself, maybe you'll come crawling back to me. And you know something, Mike?' Her mouth worked. 'I think I'll probably take you back — on my terms.'

'Liza . . . '

'Let's go home.'

She would not say another word. I thought that she was crying, yet her eyes and cheeks were dry.

When we were indoors it burst out of her. 'Damn you, Mike!' she cried; 'damn you! I hate you. You just don't know how much I hate you. I'd do anything to hurt you . . . anything. Just to hurt you the way you've hurt me.'

'I don't want to hurt you,' I tried to say. 'I want us to work it out together.'

'You've dirtied everything,' she cried.

The next day she disappeared.

4

I had no inkling of it until the evening. Liza had been at home in the morning, when I went out. We had been arguing again. At least, I had been trying to resume pleading with her, but without any success. I tried to be patient. All she had to do, I pointed out, was let me go away for the weekend to provide evidence, and then sue for divorce. There didn't have to be any hard feelings. I would make any settlement she wanted.

'Go away for your tawdry little weekend if you want to,' she said. 'I won't do a thing about it.'

'I'll have to find some other way then.' She had got to be made to realize that I meant it.

'Perhaps you can claim I've been cruel to you.'

We got nowhere. She was immovable. In the end I went out: I had to leave the flat, to get away from that hard, sneering voice. As I was on my way out she called after me:

'And you'd better do something about the Tivoli. I'm not staying there on my own.'

If I thought she meant anything definite, it was that she wouldn't go on there once I had opened with Ingrid at the Starglow Room. There was no urgency. That was something we could settle later; it was a mere side issue.

How long would it take her to see reason? A week, perhaps; perhaps even a day or two. We had quarrelled before, and each time it had come all right in the end. There always came the time when she laughed wryly and said, 'All right, all right.' Then I would make concessions, and she would make concessions, and we would find that we liked one another again.

But of course it couldn't be quite like that now. Not this time. It was hard to realize. This time there was only one concession that could break the deadlock. She was the one who had to make it.

I forced my mind on to other things. Whatever might happen at the Tivoli, there was no doubt about the future at the Starglow Room. Ingrid was going to be a smash hit there, and the sextet was going to be the most terrific thing in this country. Cool, swinging mood music. Relaxed and inventive. It would be good to sit at a keyboard again.

I spent most of the morning not so many yards from Archer Street, tracking down certain musicians I wanted. The sextet had got to be good. It had got to be the best. I dared not hope for the ideal man in every chair, but I was determined to have the best who were available. Perhaps this one could be tempted away from here, that one from there. The Caravel would fetch them.

In particular I wanted Steve Allyn on bass. He was away on a jazz club date in Glasgow, but would be back some time tomorrow.

Later on I telephoned Ingrid. Subconsciously I had been putting it off. I hadn't let myself remember to ring her — because I had nothing to tell her that I hadn't told her yesterday. I lifted the phone with apprehension — and put it down with a shameful twinge of relief when there was no reply to the insistent ringing.

I lunched alone. Yet somehow not alone. There were two of me: one yearned for Ingrid, longing to smash down the obstructions in the way; the other was reaching out into a new musical country, already half-hearing the sound of the sextet.

In the middle of the afternoon I tried again to get in touch with Ingrid. There was still no reply. I would have expected her to be in, waiting to hear from me, waiting for news. She wasn't to know that there wasn't going to be any news.

In the autumn twilight I went back to the flat. Liza was out. That, too, was a relief.

I laughed shortly. For a moment it seemed funny. I was scared of both of them at once — glad that I didn't have to speak to either of them, and tired of the whole silly business.

Then it stopped being funny. Because I wanted Ingrid. There wasn't any doubt about that.

I had a drink, and waited until it was

quite dark before switching on the lights. Already I was beginning to fidget. I had arranged that we would have a few days' relaxation when we got back from America, and now I found I was unable to relax. I wasn't used to being on my own in the evening with nothing to do. The show at the Tivoli would be beginning about now, and that was where I belonged, at any rate until we reached the Starglow Room.

The telephone rang. I snatched it up, for some reason sure that it would be Ingrid's voice.

Lew Simons said: 'Mike? Is Liza there?'

'At this time?' I said. 'She'll be at the Tivoli.'

'She's not. She hasn't shown up.'

'She must have done,' I said foolishly.

'I'm telling you she hasn't. I'm here now — I dropped in to have a word with this new song-and-dance team who're hoofing it here, and right away I get this chucked at me. Where is she?'

'I don't know. I haven't seen her all day.'

'All day?' he yelled.

'I've been out,' I said, 'contacting people for the sextet.'

'We'll be lucky if there is any sextet at the end of this. Here am I getting ready to lead up to Liza fronting the band while you sneak off to The Caravel, and now Liza isn't even here. That'll please them no end. They'll be very happy to oblige us after this, won't they?'

I said: 'She must have had an accident.' And even as I said it, I didn't believe it.

Lew groaned. 'That's all we need!' His woe grew wild and melodramatic. 'This should happen to me!' He kept a tight rein on his emotions: he had none to spare for anyone else, and if Liza had been knocked down by a bus the only pain he felt would have been a personal one. 'When did she leave?' he cried.

'I don't know. I told you I've been out all day.'

'Look,' he said. 'Look. I'll phone the police and the hospitals from this end. And I want you to get here as fast as you can make it — you and Ingrid both. If we've got any news by then, you can leave Ingrid here to do her usual numbers

58

while you go off to Liza. If she *has* had an accident, that is.'

The cunning old wretch might have been telepathic. Even along a telephone wire he could sense my doubts. But I said:

'What do you mean by that?'

'How should I know what I mean? All I know is, things aren't right between you two. The things women do . . . '

I told him to get off the line so I could phone Ingrid.

This time she was in. The first thing that hit me was the unsteadiness of her voice. I hadn't heard her like this before. She sounded as though her mouth were trembling — as though she couldn't stop it. When I had told her about Liza not reaching the Tivoli, she said, 'So she has started — I knew there would be something,' and the tremor sobbed in her throat.

'Darling, are you all right?' I demanded.

'Yes.' She must have made a great effort, but still she was not under control. 'Of course I am all right. It is nothing.'

I hesitated. Then I told her what Lew

Simons wanted us to do. Instead of upsetting her, this seemed to steady her.

'I will be ready,' she said.

'If you don't feel up to it — '

'If Liza has abdicated,' she said levelly, 'we must take over her part.'

'I'll be round as soon as I can make it,' I said.

I dressed quickly. Before I left, I looked in Liza's wardrobe. Dresses gone? I couldn't be sure. But her green suit was missing, and she would hardly have worn that if she had been going to the Tivoli. I checked in the cupboard. One of the cases was missing.

Ingrid was ready when I got to her flat. She looked haggard, but there was no trace of the unsteadiness I had detected over the phone. When I kissed her, she put her hands very lightly on my arms. I wondered how much the strain was beginning to tell on her. A rigidly controlled, undemonstrative woman, perhaps she had been suffering more than she would reveal.

As we got into the car and moved off between the clamorous lights, all exhorting people to come in to this film, that restaurant, I said:

'It looks as though Liza's gone off for a week's sulk.'

'You think it is only that?'

'She's in a pretty mad state,' I said, 'but she doesn't usually stay mad for long.'

'She may be able to keep it up for longer than a week. I told you, there is something about her. If she is willing to walk out on her contract at the Tivoli without a word, she is more than just mad.'

'She'll be back,' I said. 'Don't you worry.'

'She's clever,' said Ingrid. 'I knew she would be too clever.'

'Clever?' I echoed. 'I don't see anything so wonderfully clever in a fit of tantrums.'

'How can you divorce her,' said Ingrid, 'when you do not know where she is?'

I grabbed her hand suddenly. 'But it couldn't be better! Desertion — that's it. If she's walked out, we don't have to go through all the carefully staged weekend business, and the hired detectives. I get a divorce on grounds of desertion.'

Before she could say any more we had

arrived. Lew was waiting for us. I was angry and elated at the same time. He told us that he had checked the police and the hospitals, and as soon as he had finished I said:

'Find out for me how I get a divorce on grounds of desertion.'

'So that's it!' he moaned.

The band was playing, but the place was not yet half full. I went on stage and took over, and for twenty minutes we played for dancing. It was all straightforward stuff, but even so I noticed that the band was losing a lot of the dynamics. They needed tightening up. I would have to spend some time with them.

Behind me I could tell from the sound of the place just how it was filling up. When Ingrid came on, the tables were crowded. The applause was a sudden crashing wave. Maybe they were fond of Liza here, but they certainly weren't going to argue about Ingrid.

In an ice-blue gown under an ice-blue spot, she started with one of the numbers she had introduced just before we went to the States. It had been a hit then, and it was still a hit. *Last Night My Heart Died*, it was called. She hardly moved as she sang. In her slim remoteness, bright and lost in the middle of the floor, she was like a ghost as she lingered on the falling cadences of the tune. I was half-turned, watching her as I conducted the band. For an instant I was frightened: she looked utterly unattainable.

Then the lights brightened, the spot faded, and she moved back as though pressed towards me by the weight of the applause. She was close to me. I smiled down at her, and she gave me a quiet, satisfied little nod.

We followed up with one of the new numbers we had brought back with us. I had been going to save it, but this seemed the time and the place for its introduction.

There were no band parts yet. I went to the piano, she came up beside me, and now the spot poured down over our shoulders. Peering out of it for a moment, I saw the faces upturned; and Ingrid looked down at them, and there was still a little smile set on her lips.

I played the opening bars slow and steady — no broken tempo, no cheap flourishes for a song like this.

'I don't want to tell,' she sang, 'about the way it gets me . . . '

She was only a few inches from me. I saw the light rise and fall of her breathing. Apart from that, she was motionless until halfway through the first chorus. Then she touched her left hip casually, as though unthinkingly, with her left hand. It travelled up until it lay with the fingertips on the whiteness of her breast.

'You'll only find me doing what my conscience lets me . . . '

It was one of those songs that could have turned out dead wrong. Too much emphasis would have made it crude: you'd have felt the ripple of laughter in the audience. But I had known right from the start that it was made for Ingrid. Liza had been built up as the Sex Chill, but she had never given quite that icy perfection to a song.

I didn't want the music to finish. It was all I could do to keep myself from dragging the tempo down at the end

— anything to keep it alive, to postpone those two chords that finished it.

There was silence. And then they were shouting.

Ingrid bowed very slowly. Her left hand rested now on the piano. After a long moment she turned to me, and lifted her hand. I took it, and stood up. We both bowed. They went on shouting.

We walked off. Then we came back. It took a time before they would stop demanding the same number again. We weren't going to do it. Ingrid sang her next one against a full orchestration, and that was that for this session. Freddie, at the piano, took the band into a quickstep while we ducked out for a rest.

Lew Simons was waiting for us, looking sour and enjoying it.

He said: 'This is one hell of a time of day to be checking up on the divorce laws, but I've been doing it.'

Ingrid was rigid beside me.

'Yes?' I said.

'I could only get a rough ruling from someone I know. You'll need to check the details — '

'Go on, let's have it.'

'You can apply for a divorce on the grounds of desertion,' he said, 'after the desertion has lasted for a minimum period of three years. At the end of that time you've got to prove that the desertion was without cause, and against your wishes.'

'But — '

'If it looks as though you were glad to get rid of her anyway, it's tricky. Very tricky, so I hear. A mutual agreement to separate is an absolute stopper to divorce.'

'There's no mutual agreement,' I said.

'She's just walked out? You're sure of that?'

'It looks like it,' I said.

'You know where she's gone?'

'Not yet. I've got some ideas. I'll find out.'

'And when you find out,' said Lew, 'you're going to write to her and plead with her to come back?'

'I'm going to write to her,' I said, 'but not to ask her to come back.'

'Then you're in bad,' said Lew wearily.

'You've got to ask her to come back. Unless you ask her, and she refuses, they won't believe it's desertion.'

'This is ridiculous.' I wanted to hit someone; to smash something. 'Supposing she *isn't* anywhere I can find her? Supposing I write to her and she doesn't answer — or supposing she answers and says she *will* come back, when that's not what I want at all?'

'Better get yourself a solicitor,' rasped Lew. 'The way I see it, you're liable to find yourself having to wait seven years until you can claim she's missing — presumed dead. And even then she might bob up again, just for the hell of it.'

Seven years. I looked at Ingrid. Her mouth was set firm and unyielding. All along she had anticipated trouble.

It was too silly. I would hear from Liza tomorrow, or the day after. She had gone off to sulk. Or to think things over. She would see reason, and get in touch with me, and it would all work out all right. Liza wasn't one to plunge into melodrama.

Besides, if I wanted to find her I could

find her. England wasn't so large.

Seven years. Presumed dead . . .

I wondered where Liza was, and how much of a vindictive laugh she was getting out of the thought of this.

I had to find her.

5

I passed a restless night; and that's putting it mildly.

Ingrid had withdrawn into herself, as though once more hugging her doubts and fears and her instinctive knowledge that Liza meant trouble. We had nothing to say to one another. After all, until I could find out what had happened to Liza, there wasn't anything to say. We finished off the evening, she sang magnificently, and I dropped her at her flat on my way home.

Liza's going had left an unnerving emptiness. The flat was drained of her vitality — that overpowering energy of hers. It might have been peaceful; but in present circumstances it wasn't.

I put through a trunk call to her mother's home in Durham. It took a long time to get a reply, and when it came the answer was negative. Liza was not there. Her mother was not expecting her. Was anything wrong? I had to soothe her and say that I thought Liza might be on her way there, and I'd like to know when she arrived. But I wasn't optimistic. Running home to mother after a squabble . . . it was just too pat; it wasn't Liza at all.

Yet, if she hadn't gone home, where had she gone?

She had plenty of friends. Too many, I had often thought. I could hardly start telephoning them at this hour of the night. Tomorrow morning I would have to work it out and approach various people cautiously.

There might be no need. I might get a letter tomorrow.

It occurred to me, out of the blue, that she might have left a note for me. I spent fifteen minutes or so prowling round the flat looking for an envelope with some damn-fool farewell letter in it. There wasn't one.

I went to bed and switched the light out. After half an hour or more of tossing to and fro I sat up and put the light on again.

It wasn't that I was afraid for her. I

didn't for one moment think that she had been run over, or fallen into the Thames. Even without Lew's check on the hospitals, I knew that I wouldn't have worried along those lines. In some ways perhaps this uncertainty was worse. This was a deliberate disappearance, and much more baffling because of that.

Did that mean that I was so detached from her now that I would sooner have known her dead than simply not here?

I flinched from the thought. I got out of bed, found the whisky, and poured myself a drink.

But damn her, this was just spite — nothing else.

She'll be back tomorrow, I told myself. She'll be back, or I'll hear from her. She wants time to think it over. She's reasonable. Once she's sorted it all out in her mind . . .

I lay back, without putting the light out. Then I reached for a book from the bedside shelf.

It was a detective story, as usual. I always read detective stories. I have read so many of them — on planes and trains, in coaches driving through the night and early in the morning in provincial hotel bedrooms when the music is still twitching in my toes. In a dispassionate, couldn't-care-less sort of way I work out the permutations and spot the murderer, or think how much better it would have been if so-and-so had been the murderer.

So now, with the book open on the bed, I found myself setting up possibilities — not possibilities related to the plot of this book, but things about Liza. Suicide . . . in a fit of anguish and, even, of perverted triumph. *That'll show him*. But she would hardly have taken a case with her if she had intended to jump off Waterloo Bridge. And besides — here I went again — that just wasn't Liza. Kidnapped . . . ? No. She might be at the top of the profession, but I'd never heard of a pop singer being held for ransom.

She might have been lured out and murdered.

Nonsense.

I felt a stab of shame for being so calculating about it all, as though she were just a stock figure in a bad thriller.

But beneath the calculation was a strange dread of something I couldn't put into words. I fought it down with anger — anger against Liza for simply walking out without a word. For that's what she had really done, wasn't it? There was no question of suicide, kidnapping or murder. She had walked out, that was all.

Good riddance to her.

I have no idea what the time was when I finally got off to sleep. I woke up in the morning to find grey light through the curtains diluting the electric light which I had left on.

There were several letters in the mail, but none from Liza.

I had a breakfast that tasted like pulped clarinet reeds, and went round to see Lew. I went to his home: nothing short of the chance of booking Stan Kenton into Buckingham Palace would have got Lew to his office at this hour of the morning.

He looked terrible. His chin was bright blue, the pouches under his eyes accentuated the narrow, downward sweep of his face.

'This is a hell of a time — '

'We've got to decide what to do,' I said, brushing past him.

He slouched into the room behind me. 'We?' he said. 'I get no commission on your love-life.'

'You stand to lose a lot,' I snapped, 'if we don't get this whole business tidied up. Liza's gone. She didn't leave a message, and there was no letter this morning. She's broken her contract with the Tivoli, and — '

'And her contract with you?' said Lew smoothly.

He rubbed his chin, making a sandpapery noise, and went out of the room. He returned with an electric razor, plugged it into a socket by the mantelpiece, and began to shave.

I said: 'We've got to make some sort of announcement. It's not a thing you can keep dark, hoping she'll show up in a week's time. And I'm sure the best thing to do is to go straight at it — and make an effort to trace her quite openly.'

'Has she taken her passport with her?'

'I don't know. I haven't seen it for ages. Wouldn't know where she kept it.'

'You don't seem to have been much interested in her lately,' Lew observed, squinting at himself in the mirror.

'Look, we don't have to hedge. I want to divorce her. You know that already. But if she's disappeared — '

'You think they'll be accusing you of quietly putting her out of the way?'

That was one thing that had not crossed my mind. It wasn't a thing I was prepared to take seriously.

'That's crazy,' I said.

He cocked his head on one side and ran the razor up his jaw. 'One thing's for sure, anyway. There's not a thing you can do today. There's no reason to suspect foul play, and she's not doing anything criminal. She's old enough to walk out on you if she wants to.'

'I came round here,' I said, 'to tell you that something needed doing, and that I'm going to do it. The gossip columnists will be on to this. There'll be rumours of every kind going round before we can get our breath — and we want to be telling the same story.'

'We could always tell the plain truth.'

'I wasn't proposing anything else. But they'll start probing for the whys and wherefores. That's where we have to be careful what we say.'

Lew unplugged the shaver and rolled up the flex.

'All right. Tell me.'

'I'm going to go to the police,' I said, 'and tell them that my wife left the house yesterday without a word, and that I'm afraid she may be suffering from amnesia. The same story goes for the newspapers. I'll say how worried I am, and that I want to find her as soon as possible.'

'Sounds pretty phony to me,' said Lew dourly. 'There'll be some snide cracks about that amnesia.'

'Whichever way the news gets out, it'll start speculation.'

'I'm with you there.'

'This way we have at least got an excuse for contacting the police. They can circulate her description. The papers will publish pictures of her. Wherever she is, someone's bound to spot her, and then we'll have a lead on her.'

'She'll be so pleased,' said Lew. 'I can

just see her when some citizen dances up to her and says 'You're Liza Merriman, and I claim the *Daily Record* prize of a bucket and spade'.'

'As long as I find out where she is, that's all that matters.'

He stuffed his hands into the pockets of his lurid dressing-gown, and stared at me like an accusing judge.

'Don't plunge straight into it,' he said.

'But I've got to find her.'

'At any rate, ring some of her friends up first. I don't see why you didn't just stay at home ringing everyone this morning, instead of getting me up at this time.'

'Because there are liable to be reporters sniffing round,' I retorted. 'I'm surprised none of the morning papers had any mention of it. The evening ones will be on the trail all right — and I don't intend to be at home until I've got everything straight.'

'All right. Go to my office, then, and do some telephoning.'

'There isn't much time before the newspaper boys get cracking.'

'At least *try* before you go shouting the story to the whole wide world.'

'All right,' I said, 'I'll try.'

★   ★   ★

On my way to Lew's office, it suddenly occurred to me to drop in and see Dave Blair. It only meant a small detour. It was a wild shot — I'd never had any reason to suppose that Liza was ever prepared to fall into Dave's arms — but I remembered how anxious she had been to go to his club that evening when we talked, and how he had looked at the two of us.

He was out of bed, but only just. He looked frowsty, as Lew had done. We all belonged to a night world; the morning was an alien territory.

His flat was a pitiful place compared with Lew's. Or compared with my own, if it came to that. It was a couple of rooms and a poky kitchen with a wooden table-top resting over the bath. Dave lived on his own. At one time and another there had been women here with him, but none of them lasted long. The stale, enclosed smell of the place hit me as he waved me towards a decrepit armchair; and I found myself trying to detect, through it, just a trace of Liza's perfume. Had she come here for refuge?

Dave, rubbing his hand along his bristly jaw in a gesture that echoed Lew's, said:

'If you've come here to offer me that job again, the answer is still no.'

'That's not what I've come for.'

'I thought you couldn't be that desperate.'

I said: 'I'm looking for Liza.'

He stared. I wondered if he was stalling and trying to play the innocent. But in my bones I already felt that she wasn't here.

'You mean you've gone and mislaid her?' he said harshly. If he had meant it to sound funny, he failed.

'She's gone,' I said. 'Disappeared. I'm worried.'

'What the hell made you think she'd come here?'

'It was only a chance. I want to find her, and I don't know where to start.'

He perched on the edge of a couch still

littered with yesterday's papers. 'You asked for it,' he said.

'She may have had a blackout — loss of memory, or something like that.'

Dave laughed. It was not a happy sound.

'Much more likely to be the opposite,' he said. 'The dawn of reason, rather than loss of memory, if you ask me. Didn't she leave any message?'

'None.'

'If she *had* come here,' he said, 'she'd have got better treatment than she seems to have had from you in recent times.'

'Since she isn't here, I'll get moving.'

He got up. 'Sure you wouldn't like to look round the place just to make sure?'

I said: 'Dave, if she should happen to contact you — '

'You want her to come home?'

'Naturally I want to know where she is,' I said.

'Ah, I see.' He held the door open for me, and there was nothing friendly about him. 'I doubt whether she'll contact me,' he said. 'I imagine she's hiding out somewhere, licking her wounds. If she ever does come back, it'll be in her own good time.'

'I'm going to find her,' I said. 'I'll have her traced somehow.'

'You're going to make yourself look a bit of a fool.'

'I can handle it all right,' I assured him.

He was about to shut the door behind me, then stopped for a moment. 'Why not leave her alone?' he said. 'If she wants to go off for a rest from you, give the girl some peace.'

Then he shut the door.

I went along to Lew's office. He had already telephoned his secretary, and she let me into his inner room. I started making calls. In the middle of one, I would scribble down another name as it occurred to me.

First of all I got in touch with Liza's mother again, just to make sure. Liza had not shown up. Her mother was worried now. I told her that I was worried, too, but that I was taking steps to find Liza. She would be all right, but she might have had a temporary lapse of memory. If any word did come from her, I would like to know about it, no matter how brief or apparently uninformative it was.

Then I tried several of Liza's friends. I made it sound as casual as I could. 'I've got to get in touch with her before the show this evening,' I said, 'and she's gone out without letting me know where she'll be. I just thought she might have arranged to meet you . . . ' One of them had already heard a whisper. 'I heard she wasn't at the Tivoli last night,' she said eagerly. 'Had a tiff, Mike?' I kept it non-committal, but I could imagine that particular woman beaming when she saw the papers, and saying, 'I told you so,' to herself — if, that is, she didn't get round to telling a lot of other people as well.

In the middle of the afternoon I went to the police.

They knew me fairly well at the local station. Once they had recovered my car when it had been stolen, and on two occasions they had been regrettably firm over a little matter of speeding. This time I met a new character. When I had explained my problem, the man at the desk shook his head and said: 'This sounds like one for the D.D.I., sir.'

The D.D.I. had a very black moustache, and the sort of wrinkles men get round their eyes when they have lived in a hot climate for years.

'I understand you want to report somebody as missing, sir?' He had a resonant voice, tinged with a permanent scepticism.

'My wife,' I said.

'Perhaps you would give me the details.'

I gave him the details. I got the impression that he was not taking me very seriously.

'What makes you think your wife is missing, sir?' He smiled thoughtfully, not at me but at the end of his pencil. 'I mean, she only left yesterday. Women often clear off for a day or two in a huff. It doesn't do to get too steamed up right away. You'd had a disagreement about something, perhaps?'

'Nothing of any consequence,' I said.

'M'm. But we know what women are, don't we? It may have been of consequence to her at the time.'

He waited. He had an air of being ready to hear what the disagreement had been about. I thought it unwise to say that we had been arguing about divorce and that I wanted to find my wife so that I could persuade her to divorce me. It was unlikely that the police would view such proposed collusion very favourably.

In the end he went on: 'I'd give it a few more days, if I were you, sir. Saturday tomorrow, you know. She'll probably stay away over the weekend and then come back nice and calmed down. Unless, that is' — the eyes sunk between the wrinkles were abruptly bright and sharp — 'you've some good reason for supposing there's more to it than that.'

'I'm worried,' I said.

'You understand, sir, that we're . . . h'm . . . rather limited in our scope. I mean . . . ' He coughed. 'I ought to point out that if it's a question of — well, say, another man . . . anything like that . . . it's up to you to institute civil proceedings . . . '

'My wife has not run away with another man,' I said stiffly.

'You're sure of that, sir?'

'As nearly as makes no odds,' I said.

'I hope you won't mind my putting it like this — only trying to help . . . But you have, I believe, been away in America for a couple of months. While you've been away, there's always the chance . . . '

'No,' I said.

'Very good, sir. Why *do* you think she's disappeared, then?'

'I can't tell. If I could, I might have some lead to go on. But I've got a feeling she may have had some temporary loss of memory.'

'She has had them before?'

'Not exactly,' I said. 'But' — this was the way I had decided to put it — 'she has always been highly strung. She's had a lot of responsibility these last weeks, with my being away in America.'

He nodded, but without much conviction.

Suddenly I saw it. I said: 'I can't help feeling that malicious newspaper gossip has had a lot to do with it. You know what these gossip writers are like.'

'They can be indiscreet,' he said smoothly.

'They've been printing a lot of guesses about myself and a new singer I've engaged. It's the sort of thing that goes on all the time, and it may have preyed on my wife's mind. She was certainly upset about it all.'

'Yes. I see.'

It was not an encouraging session. I felt absurdly as though I had been put in the dock to answer a lot of awkward questions, and it was only afterwards that I wondered whether the inspector had really been entitled to ask them. But at the end he did at any rate take down the address of Liza's mother, and some brief details of Liza's recent movements. I supplied him with several photographs, and gave him as full a description of her as I could. That was the oddest part of it: I felt unaccountably shaky as I described her eyes and her hair, the way she moved her shoulders as she walked, and the green suit she had probably been wearing when she went away.

'We'll do what we can, sir,' he said as I was leaving, 'but we'll have to be very discreet. You do realize that if Mrs.

Merriman was in full possession of her faculties when she left, and is annoyed at being disturbed now, we shall have to explain that you reported her quite definitely as missing.'

'Of course I realize that,' I said. 'That's what I came here for. I want to find her.'

'Yes, of course,' he said.

★　★　★

News travelled fast. There were two reporters at the Tivoli when I got there. I told them the same story I had told the police, and did my best to keep them away from Ingrid.

There was very little I could say to Ingrid. Her refusal to demand anything made it worse. If she had raged at me, or broken down into tears, I might have been able to shout my way through the confusion in my own mind.

Instead, we went through the performance. We played, she sang, and the audience lapped it up. The second alto in the band was not up to form: he looked pale before we started, and fluffed several notes during the course of the evening; any other time, I'd have given him hell, but at the moment I had too much to think about.

Looking at the dancers on the floor, or at the upturned faces when the cabaret was on, I realized that there were too many things at stake. If Liza did not come back, our chances of getting into the Starglow Room were small. The Tivoli would hardly release me unless they had Liza in my place. That had been part of Lew's tentative arrangement.

Liza had well and truly bitched everything.

I looked at Ingrid as she sang. We had come so close together; was she now, after all, to drift away from me again?

Somehow we reached the end of the evening. I noticed that Cy Mitchell, the second alto, was trembling convulsively as he put his sax away. I was about to go and have a word with him — he looked feverish to me — when Freddie came over from the piano and said:

'Don't forget tomorrow morning, boss.'

'Tomorrow?'

'We've got a broadcast to record.'

'My God. I *had* forgotten.'

'If you want me to take over . . . '

'No. I'll have to be in on it.'

I would, too. It was a special feature that had been fixed before we went away. A welcome home programme after the American tour. Welcome home, Mike Merriman. Welcome home, Ingrid Lee. Bye-bye, Liza Merriman.

'Thanks for reminding me, Freddie,' I said. 'And now there's another favour I'd like you to do me. Will you grab a cab and take Ingrid home? I have a feeling some of those press busybodies may be hanging around. I don't want any fancy slants in those newspaper stories tomorrow.'

'Sure thing.'

'Poke any intruders in the mug,' I said. 'I'll bail you out and pay your costs.'

I went home alone. The flat was still empty, still the same — only emptier, if that was possible.

Tonight I took a sleeping pill. I didn't want to lie awake again, dreaming up melodramas. I found I didn't even want to think about Ingrid. It was too tantalizing. I just didn't want to think at all.

* * *

Two of the morning papers made a minor splash over Liza's disappearance. Three others reported it briefly. The others ignored it; but they were all capable of making a big thing of it at the drop of a hat, if the circumstances warranted.

In the noisiest of them all there was a feature about Ingrid and myself alongside the news story of Liza's disappearance. The two were only loosely connected, but the implications were cleverly made. There was a brief account of Liza's marriage to me and her build-up as the Sex Chill. There was a photograph of Liza, and beside it a photograph of Ingrid, both wearing similar gowns and gazing out over a microphone into the middle distance. FROM FREEZING POINT DOWNWARDS, the feature was headed. There was a brief review of Ingrid's merits as a singer, tied up with reports on the American tour. 'We used to call it torch singing,' wrote the reviewer, 'but Miss Lee's flame is a cold one. 'Cool' jazz has got ice on it these days.' There were no real facts about Ingrid, because no facts had ever been released. We had kept her mysterious. In fact, she had kept herself mysterious. There had been none of that backstreet-to-neon-lights stuff. Ingrid had been a goddess from the start. It suited the public — and, in a way I could never get round to explaining to myself, it suited me, too.

Today the publicity didn't look quite so good, set alongside that account of Liza walking out.

Loss of memory ... possibility of accident not ruled out ...

Lew was right. It sounded phony.

But that didn't matter, if it drew people's attention to her, so that some-one, somewhere, recognized her and put us on the trail.

I had the whole batch of papers with me when I reached the studio. The familiar bleat of the band tuning up rasped horribly. The idea of sleek music was wrong at this time of day. I groaned, and tossed the papers on a chair. Ingrid glanced at them and glanced away.

I said: 'Have you seen — '

'Yes,' she said, 'I saw the article.'

'It's a bloody mess.'

She touched my hand lightly, brushing it with light fingers. 'There is time,' she said. 'You will find a way.'

That sounded fine.

We started the recording session. The heartiness of the announcer jarred on me. It would have jarred on anybody. Quite apart from anything else, it was the wrong tone for our sleek music. Everything ought to have been played down. I had taken years to develop this suave, insinuating music, and nothing could wreck the mood more easily than this sort of boisterous good-fellowship.

'And I understand, Mike' — I'd never met the man before, but the script said 'Mike' so he called me that — 'that you've brought a couple of terrific new numbers back from the States with you.'

I looked at my script. 'That's right, John,' I said. 'The first of them . . . '

I reeled the words off without troubling

to consider whether they made sense. It was all unreal this morning. A session like this was never the same as a live broadcast, anyway. I wondered fleetingly whether, if it had been a live broadcast, I would have been able to bring myself to burst out with a wild appeal to Liza to play fair, to come back and carry on at the Tivoli and . . . talk things over. She would have got a great kick out of that!

When it was over and we were packing up, I went across to Ingrid. I wanted to be alone with her. I wanted to get out of here and be with her, so that I could be sure she was real and that everything was going to be cleared up.

'Let's get out of here,' I said.

Thoughtfully she shook her head.

'I think we should not be seen together for a little while.' She spoke like a child who has been meticulously learning a lesson. 'I . . . I cannot bear to think of anything going wrong, Mike.'

I wanted to put my arms round her. She was more vulnerable than I had thought. In spite of her reluctance, I took her arm and guided her towards the door.

'To hell with them all,' I said.

'No.' She freed herself gently as we emerged into the open air. 'I know I am right. I'll see you at the Tivoli. But outside, I think it is better to be careful — not to encourage the gossips.'

Of course she was right. But I wanted to hold on to her and not let her go.

'They'll find Liza,' I said desperately.

'Of course. We must be patient.'

'No one who looks like Liza can hide away. Not in this country. Those pictures in the paper, and the descriptions that have been issued of her . . . '

'Darling, we can hardly hope for her to go around in public obligingly wearing her green suit and jade earrings.'

'Changing her clothes won't make her all that unrecognizable,' I said.

'A woman can make herself quite unrecognizable that way if she wishes,' said Ingrid with the trace of a smile.

I tried to smile back. 'Maybe. In this case I'm hoping not.'

I went back to the flat before lunch, just in the stubborn hope that there might be a letter in the latter post. I carried the newspapers back with me, and when there was no post I sat down and read through the crudely malicious news stories again.

Then I was conscious of a nagging suspicion at the back of my mind. I began to go through the papers one by one — very, very slowly.

When I had finished, and was quite sure, I went through to the bedroom and opened the top two drawers of Liza's dressing-table. I searched them systematically. Then I looked round the room to make sure there was nowhere else. But I had known all along that this was where the things would be if she had left them behind.

The jade earrings that I had given Liza — the last present I had bought her, immediately before leaving for America — were missing. Ingrid had mentioned them: Ingrid had spoken of them in conjunction with the green suit that Liza had almost certainly been wearing when she left.

But in the description I had given to the police, and the description which appeared in the newspapers, there was no mention of jade earrings.

6

I tried to telephone Ingrid. There was no reply. I went to a little place round the corner for a lunch that I didn't even taste, and then I came back and tried another call. There was still no reply.

In the afternoon I tried to settle down to some new orchestrations. It was time the band had some fresh material. Eight weeks was a long time to be away in this racket: tunes changed and tastes were liable to change if you didn't keep the public satisfied — and stimulated.

I sketched out what you might call a typical Merriman introduction. Eight bars of beautifully suave, thickly harmonized stuff that led in to a solo by a long muted trombone. It was just right. I introduced a pleasantly jarring flattened ninth. I could hear the whole thing in my mind: it was Merriman music, without a doubt.

It was terrible.

I sat and stared at the sheet of manuscript. What I had done was perfectly all right, but I didn't like it and I couldn't go on.

The title of the number was *I'm a Woman with a Plan*. I sat and stared at that, too.

What, after all, did I know about Ingrid, apart from the taste of her mouth and the joy of looking at her and listening to that insidiously beautiful voice of hers? She had told me she had no ties — she was an orphan, she had lived for some years with an aunt in the north, and she had come to London because it was one of the things most girls wanted to do. 'I have nobody,' she had said simply; and that was pretty well that. She had nobody, but she never seemed lonely. Perhaps that self-possession of hers masked a driving force that I had been too stupid to see. Perhaps she had planned from the start to get rid of Liza and take her place?

To get rid of Liza . . .

I blinked, and sat back. What had got into me? If this was love — suspecting Ingrid of . . . well, of what?

The score of that number had got no further than the introductory eight bars when I left for the Tivoli that evening. I went along early, to have a word with Ingrid before we started. I wanted to have it settled.

She was late. We were all ready to start when she arrived. There was no time for talk now.

Saturday was always a crowded night. There was more noise than usual, and the brass section put more weight into things, to cut through the babble. The inevitable crop of drunks shrieked and whistled at the cabaret acts. Some of them howled at Ingrid when she came on, but she did not falter. Within a matter of seconds after she had begun to sing she had silenced them.

I watched her. I wanted to get her away from the microphone and drag the truth out of her. But now I found it impossible to imagine what sort of answer she would give when I spoke to her. It wasn't easy to be suspicious of her when she was right there in front of me.

It was Clyde Goff, the drummer, who

had found her. Was he in on some funny business? The two of them, perhaps, had fixed it that he would arouse my interest, get me to go along and see the girl, take her on . . .

That didn't fit. Clyde hadn't made a big thing out of it. He had mentioned her, and more or less by chance I had dropped in and heard her. I had offered her the chance, and she had seized it.

Oh, yes, she had seized it. She had known exactly what to do — singing magnificently, holding herself aloof from me and playing hard to get until Liza was out of the way . . . perhaps doing more than I had realized to *get* Liza out of the way . . .

As soon as the interval began, and the trio took over from us on the stand, I went into the tiny room she shared with two of the women in the floor show.

'Come and have a drink,' I said.

'That would be nice.'

We stood in the corridor beside the band-room, because there was nowhere else we could keep away from people. A cold draught blew along it, oddly tinged with the warm smell of cooking and cigarette smoke.

I said: 'I've been wondering about Liza.'

'Oh! Oh, yes.'

'I've been wondering,' I said with difficulty, 'what made you mention the jade earrings she was wearing the day she left.'

Ingrid stood quite still. After a moment she said: 'There is something wrong?'

'How did you know she was wearing jade earrings?' I asked.

'It . . . no, I am not sure. It was in the papers.'

'It wasn't. No mention of it.'

'There must have been.'

'There couldn't have been. I was the one who issued the description — and until you mentioned the earrings I hadn't even thought of them. I checked up this morning, and they're missing. Very likely she's wearing them, as you said; but how did *you* know?'

Freddie came out of the band-room and brushed his plump body along the wall. There was plenty of room in the corridor for him to pass, but Freddie had a thing about his fatness: he always tried to flatten himself against one wall or the other, as though there could not possibly be space for himself and anybody else abreast.

''Scuse me, boss.'

Two girls in a small quantity of feathers came along from the opposite direction.

When they had passed, Ingrid said: 'I must have seen Liza wearing them some other time, and it stayed in my memory.'

'That won't do either,' I said grimly.

'Mike, you are so angry. Mike, what is it?'

She lifted her hand as though to shield her eyes. Her arm was smooth and white. I felt weak, but still very angry. She was right about that.

I said: 'I gave those earrings to Liza just before we left for the States. She couldn't have worn them before we went. You couldn't possibly have seen them.'

'What are you saying?'

'I'm saying that you saw Liza on the day she disappeared.'

Her arm fell to her side. Faintly in the

distance we could hear the trio, playing a fast number that tinkled away like a far-off barrel-organ.

I waited. Freddie came back, and wriggled close to the wall again.

'Well?' I said.

She looked for somewhere to put her empty glass. I took it from her and put it with mine, on a ledge above our heads.

'Yes,' she said. 'It is true. I saw Liza.'

'But why the blazes — '

'I . . . did not like to tell you. There was so much to worry about. Already you have too much. And it was so . . . so unpleasant.' She shivered, as though the draught had, for the first time, stung her bare shoulders.

'Tell me,' I said.

'It was nothing much. Just unpleasant.'

'Tell me.'

She began to walk slowly down the corridor. I fell into step beside her.

'You tried to telephone me that morning, didn't you?' she began.

'Did I?' I thought back. 'Yes, of course. I wanted to tell you what had happened between Liza and myself the previous evening.' I could still recall the feeling of relief when there was no reply, because I had had so little that was good to tell.

'I thought it was you. I had been sitting in, waiting for you to ring. But Liza came. That was why I did not answer. She guessed it was you. I saw it in her face. We sat there and let it ring, and when it stopped we went on talking.'

We turned, and came back along the corridor. There was a bumble of voices from the band-room, and Clyde was laughing his high, hysterical laugh.

'What did you talk about?' I prompted her.

'About you, of course.' Her hand found mine and held it for a moment, then let go. 'It was . . . not nice. Liza told me that she hated me. She said I was not good enough for you, and that we would not be happy together. You might almost say' — she forced a smile — 'that she *promised* me we would not be happy.'

'What did you do?'

'I wanted to do something for her. I felt guilty . . . '

'No reason why you should. You didn't

ask me to fall in love with you.'

'It's not as easy as that,' murmured Ingrid. 'It was because of me that she was unhappy, and if I could have done anything . . . But I was not going to give you up. She came to talk to me, and try to persuade me, but I couldn't help her. I had to ask her to go — I told her it was no use. And she said . . . '

'Yes?'

'I remember her words,' said Ingrid slowly, 'and the way she said them. She said: 'One of us has got to go. For the time being, it's got to be me. But I'll be back.' That was what she said, Mike. 'I'll be back,' she said, 'and by that time I don't think you'll still be around, Ingrid'.'

The anger was still there, burning away inside me. But now it was back where it belonged: it was the old anger against Liza. I could imagine her going round to pit herself against Ingrid. I could almost hear her.

I said: 'I know Liza. I don't believe that that was all she said to you, Ingrid. Darling, that wasn't all, was it?'

'Darling . . . '

'I'll bet there was plenty more. The bitch. Even when she was all set to walk out, she had to do as much damage as possible before going.'

There was no time to say more. Our next stint was due to begin, and the boys were sauntering out of their room.

For the remainder of the evening we played well. Or maybe it was just that my mind was only now free to appreciate just how good the band was. I particularly noticed that Cy Mitchell, whose alto blowing had been so painful the night before, was really in the mood. His couple of solo spots were carried off with an intonation and limpid ease that would have made Charlie Parker sit up in his grave and take notice. I nodded at him. His lips parted in a jubilant grin on either side of his mouthpiece. He was living every note that he played, and he was living it up good. Everything was just right, for all of us.

Ingrid sang again, and again she had the audience where she wanted them. I was part of that audience. I watched her just as greedily as all the other men there.

The difference was that soon I would be within reach of fulfilment of the dream that they were all of them dreaming. Looking at her body, sheathed in its white gown, I was in a mood to give Liza plenty of grounds for divorcing me, plenty of evidence. But what was the good, when she wasn't around to act on it?

When we went out that night there were two heavy-eyed reporters waiting. They looked pretty despairing; there must have been a shortage of good material for the Sunday papers.

'Any story for us yet, Mr. Merriman?'

'No news yet? What do you think about the disappearance, Miss Lee? It hasn't affected your singing . . . ?'

Freddie was behind us, mincing carefully down the two steps so that he did not block anyone's exit.

I said: 'When we get to the car, Freddie . . . '

'Right, boss. I'll take her. Do I get any overtime pay?'

I moved away from Ingrid, awkwardly, trying too late to make it clear that there was nothing between us. The reporters wavered, watching us separate and not sure which way to jump.

It was because I was a few feet away from her that I saw Ingrid's instinctive tremor. She stopped. Her eyes widened.

I followed the direction of her gaze. At the end of the alley, in the shadows, there was a darker shadow. The old lamp on the back wall of the Tivoli cast a slanting ray of light. It picked out the face of someone on the corner for a moment. Then the face was gone, and the shadow crossed the end of the alley. It looked like a woman.

Ingrid turned towards Freddie, waiting for him I moved across to her.

'What is it?' I asked in an undertone.

The reporters came closer again.

'Nothing,' she said.

'You looked scared.' It seemed a ridiculous thing to say about Ingrid.

'It was nothing,' she insisted.

7

Two weeks passed. There was no sign of Liza, and no word from her. The inspector with the black moustache and the tight, probing eyes came to see me twice. I discovered that his name was Manton, and that's about all I did discover. On both occasions he repeated his earlier performance of making me feel that I was in the dock. After he had gone the second time, it struck me with a shock that he had been asking the sort of question one would associate with a murder enquiry. He might even be wondering whether I had killed Liza. From the way some of the papers had played the story up for a few days, that was hardly surprising — but it wasn't comfortable.

The papers had given up now. There had been no further news, and the possibilities of carefully slanted gossip had been exhausted. We were left alone.

I had another reason, now, for hating Liza. The job at The Caravel had fallen through. Lew did his best, but he couldn't swing it with the Tivoli management.

'If Liza shows up again soon, that's O.K.,' he explained. 'Might even be good publicity. But they won't let you out of the contract otherwise. If Liza's not here, you've got to lead the band, Mike.'

The sound of the sextet came back into my head like a tantalizing echo. I thought of the music we might have made. But Liza had gone, and I was stuck with the Tivoli engagement.

And I was stuck with the responsibility of being cautious in my meetings with Ingrid.

For myself, I'd have been willing to thumb my nose at the whole blasted world. Let the gossip writers warm up again. Let people say things behind my back about the odd way that Liza had disappeared. Let the whole lot of them do whatever they liked, so long as Ingrid and I were together. But she held me to her original proposal: she was right in wanting us to tread warily, and I knew she was right, but it didn't help. Was I to stand no chance of possessing her until Liza had been found?

We drove out into Kent one Sunday and had a meal. We talked about where we would live when we were married, and she described the sort of house she wanted. It was cool and fresh and lightly romantic, but it wasn't enough. I said:

'I can't go on much longer, Ingrid.'

She studied me with a long, slow, unblinking stare. You would have thought either that she had not understood or that she enjoyed my impatience and intended to keep me impatient. But her voice was melancholy.

'You're tired of me, Mike?'

'You know damn well what I mean. I can't go on waiting, wasting time, when I want you so much.'

'You will have me,' she said.

'I don't want to wait for Liza to show up,' I said. 'We're grown-up, we know what we're doing — this isn't the nineteenth century.'

'I want it to be right,' she said with her

terrible, simple earnestness. 'It must be just right. And then . . . it will be perfect. You will see.'

I lay awake that night, as I had done so many other nights, and in my mind I called her dirty names. And then I called her other names, and longed for her.

For all the good it did.

The stupid, adolescent, sentimental thing about it was that I agreed with her. In spite of the gnawing physical pain of it — the awful clamour of it inside me — I knew what she meant, and I wanted it the way she wanted it. Liza would have laughed. I fought down the memory of her cheap sneers.

But it had to be soon. I couldn't wait for ever. I couldn't go on standing there in front of the band every night while Ingrid sang; I couldn't go on watching the lift of her breasts and the way her hand brushed her hip, and still be good and patient like some drab young bank clerk adding up the months until he could afford to be formally, respectably married.

In the space of a few weeks about two

hundred people wrote to me to tell me where Liza was. They had seen her. They were all wrong. The police followed up several trails of their own and arrived nowhere.

The nights were growing dark and wretched. It seemed that we emerged every night after the show into streets shining with rain.

We played the old numbers, and the new ones as they came along. They all began to sound the same. One evening I got frightened. I seemed to be standing outside myself and asking questions. Here I was, at the top of the tree, playing the sort of music I had devised myself and making one hell of a big success of it — and what did it mean? I wasn't aiming to be deeply philosophical about it. I just wanted to know why I wasn't getting a kick out of things the way I used to.

It would be different when I had Ingrid.

I determined to talk to her afterwards. No matter what she said, we were going to go on and have a talk after the show. I was conscious, from the corner of my eye, of her slim brightness as she sang. Faces were upturned. I wanted her to myself, away from all the faces and the grasping, mass desire.

Often she was ready to leave before I was, and nowadays she did not wait for Freddie. I hurried after her when we had finished.

'Ingrid, don't go. I want to see you.'

'Darling, I'm so tired.'

'You're going to listen to me,' I said.

The place was too full and too noisy. While I was getting my coat she slipped away.

I hastened down the corridor, leaving the boys packing up and talking. As I came out of the door at the back of the building, I could hear spasms of voices from the end of the alley, as people went home or shouted across the street or asked where a car had got to or when the devil they were going to get a taxi.

There was no sign of Ingrid until I looked the other way. Even then I had a moment's doubt. There were two shadows — very still. They might have been due only to the high walls and slanting light at the dead end of the alley. Then there was the hiss of a voice, and the movement of an arm.

I took a couple of steps towards the shadows, and stopped.

Ingrid had her back to the wall. The woman in front of her had a cloak about her shoulders — or else it was a coat loosely flung over the shoulders. The upraised arm looked as though it were about to descend and smash across Ingrid's face.

I said: 'What the hell is going on?'

'Don't move, Mike,' said Ingrid very quietly. I could see her eyes faintly now, as the light caught them. She was not looking at me. She stared straight into the threatening shadow before her. 'Don't do anything,' she said. 'She has . . . vitriol.'

The upraised arm trembled slightly. Or perhaps that was another trick of the shadows.

'Liza,' I whispered, 'you're crazy. Put it down.'

She did not even glance at me. The whole tableau was fixed and unalterable. I wished someone else would come out of the door behind me. The spasmodic noises of the street were far away.

I moved forward.

'No,' cried Ingrid, breaking suddenly and putting her arm across her face.

There was a sudden laugh, right on top of her cry. The shadows split up, I was pushed aside, and the cloak swirled past.

I pursued her as far as the end of the alley. 'Don't!' Ingrid was crying behind me. 'Leave her, Mike!' But I emerged into the brightness of the street, and the crowds were still milling to and fro, surging out towards taxis and cars. It was no good.

I turned and went back. Ingrid seized my arms, and her fingers bit in.

'Mike.'

She clung desperately to me as I kissed her.

I said: 'She must have gone mad. Ingrid — it *was* Liza, wasn't it?'

She buried her face in my shoulder, trembling. 'If you had seen her face . . . Yes, it was Liza all right. And she is mad.'

8

There was a poster for a police ball tacked up on the back of Manton's door. An ancient calendar with a big picture of a sad-looking retriever hung askew on the wall behind his desk. Manton himself looked about as excited as though we had come to report the loss of a charm bracelet.

'Are you making a definite accusation against your wife, Mr. Merriman?'

'What else do you suppose I'm doing?'

'You're prepared to swear it was her?' His gaze flickered peremptorily towards Ingrid.

She said: 'It was Liza.'

'You say she threatened you with sulphuric acid?'

'She told me that the bottle she had in her hand contained vitriol, and that I must stand still.'

'But she didn't throw it at you?'

I said: 'I came out just in time.'

'From what you've told me,' said Manton, 'she had plenty of time in which to throw it and get away. If she'd wanted to, that is.'

It was something I had been telling myself all night. Now I said: 'You mean she was only trying to frighten Miss Lee? She had no intention of using the stuff?'

'It may have been just a bottle of water,' said Manton.

Ingrid said: 'I think it is true. She meant only to frighten me. I did not want us to come to the police about it.'

'Oh?' Manton never let his eyes wander, as most people do when they are talking. His gaze was rigid, moving as though on a swivel. 'Why not, Miss Lee?'

'This morning, when I thought it over, I knew that it was not real. She would not have thrown the vitriol.'

'It certainly sounds rather melodramatic in the cold light of morning,' Manton agreed. 'There's something terribly old-fashioned about it. You still get cases on the Continent, but in all my years on this job I've never heard of a case in this country. Only someone unbalanced — '

'That's just it,' I broke in. 'If my wife is

117

unbalanced enough to indulge in melodramatic gestures like that, she may be
capable of going further. Last night her
nerve may have failed her at the last
minute. She was interrupted, and perhaps
it shook her. Next time we may not be so
lucky. Miss Lee is trying to play the whole
thing down this morning, but I still think
we've got to do something about it.'

'What do you want doing?'

I said: 'Before, it was simply a case of
my wife's disappearing. Nothing criminal
in that. Now you've got a much better
reason for looking for her. She threatened
to attack Miss Lee. Don't tell me that's
not an offence?'

'Threats and menaces,' Manton nodded.
'Action which may lead to a breach of the
peace. Oh, yes, there's a case against Mrs.
Merriman.'

'You've got to find her.'

'We've already looked for her,' said
Manton, 'and there's been a lot of
publicity. She hasn't shown up. It would
be difficult to intensify the search. And
are you sure you want us to?'

'Good God, man!'

'The publicity could be dangerous. People would crowd around Miss Lee wherever she went, hoping for something to happen. Believe me, I know. And the attacker could all too easily mingle with crowds like that.'

'I want a permanent guard on Miss Lee,' I said. 'You can provide that, can't you, without making too much fuss about it?'

Manton sucked the edge of his moustache with his lower lip. 'H'm. If we put a guard on everyone who has been vaguely threatened we'd need twice the number of men we've got. You'd be surprised how many husbands and wives make a practice of threatening one another with choppers, breadknives and blunt instruments. And even when we do take it seriously we don't stand much chance of stopping the actual assault. That's how it would be this time. If Mrs. Merriman does attack Miss Lee we'd pull her in after the attack, but the odds against our being able to foresee it are pretty small.'

'Quite a defeatist,' I said.

'Mr. Merriman, do *you* know when your wife will make her next move against Miss Lee — if she makes one at all? Do you know the direction it'll come from, the time of day it's likely to happen, exactly where it will take place . . . ?'

Ingrid said: 'I must be ready for the next one. That is all we can do.'

He nodded. At last there was some expression in his eyes: it was admiration. 'That's it, Miss Lee.' The admiration seemed to work wonders. He went on: 'I tell you what we'll try, though. I'll detail a plain clothes man to keep close behind you during the day, for a fortnight. We can't spare one longer than that. If you want anything more, you'll have to engage a private detective. At the same time I'll arrange for the man on the beat to keep an eye on your place at night. And it's up to you to take every possible precaution of your own — locking up, keeping alert, not being alone any more than you can help.'

I said: 'And after all that, it only takes one bullet fired from the audience any night at the Tivoli — '

'No power on earth can stop that, Mr. Merriman. Even if the management searched every customer at the door on the way in, a really determined person could find some way of smuggling a weapon in and taking a pot shot. There's no fool-proof way of staying alive if somebody's after you in dead earnest. You've just got to do the best you can.'

Ingrid's fears of the night before seemed to have gone. She had been shuddering when I put my arms round her in that shadowed alley, but now she was calm again. She smiled at the inspector, as though to assure him that he didn't have to worry about my fussiness.

We supplied him with as complete a programme of Ingrid's movements as possible before we left. It was arranged that I would pick her up every evening before the show, and go back with her each night. Newspaper gossip writers could make what they chose of it, so long as they did not get any inkling of the truth. A plain clothes man would telephone Ingrid every morning at eleven o'clock to see what her plans were for the day. If she intended to go out for a meal or to do any shopping, he would come round before she set out and follow her.

Driving away, I said: 'There's one way of saving ourselves all these complications.'

'What, darling?'

'You could come and live with me,' I said.

'Not yet.'

'To hell with the lot of them,' I said. 'What would it matter? If Liza finds out, so much the better. Maybe it will drive her to divorce me. We've been too fussy by half about the possible scandal. Let them talk. Nobody cares, in our line of business.'

She did not answer. I had to concentrate on slinking through a particularly imbecilic traffic jam, and then it was only a matter of minutes to her door.

When I got out I motioned her to stay where she was for a moment. I felt an unpleasant prickling at the back of my neck as I stood beside the car, looking along the road. It appeared perfectly normal, but I remembered all too vividly what Manton had said. What direction would an attack come from? The time of day, the place . . .

There were the usual parked cars, the usual men and women walking along the pavement. A hundred windows looked down on us. Liza might be behind any one of them.

I forced myself to walk round and open the door on Ingrid's side. Her sleek silken leg flashed, her hand rested in mine, and she was out and standing up, almost in my arms. I thought of a bullet smashing that beautiful head, or acid disfiguring that face, and I felt myself shivering uncontrollably.

We went in together.

Ingrid poured us a drink. I seemed to need one more than she did.

I took up where I had left off. 'We've got to live together. It's the obvious way.'

'You think that would be a happy way to begin?' she said gently. 'A married life started in fear — lying awake listening to noises in the night, waiting for someone to strike?'

'Better that,' I said, 'than leaving you to

wait on your own.'

'No,' she said. 'No, my dear.'

I put my glass down. I went over and kissed her. She kept her eyes open, and put one hand very lightly on my chest. Then her lips opened. I went down beside her, and put my left hand on her breast. Her mouth murmured under mine. She pushed against me, trying to force me back, but I knocked her arm out of the way, and she did not bring it back again.

'I love you,' I said.

'I love to hear you say it,' she whispered.

The telephone began to ring.

'Leave it,' I said.

But she slid past me, her hair brushing my cheek. She lifted the receiver.

I sighed, and got up. Then I saw her face.

'What is it?' I demanded. I put my hand out, wanting to take the receiver from her. She paid no attention.

The voice at the other end was inaudible from where I stood. All Ingrid said was, 'Yes,' and then, very slowly, 'I am not frightened.' She listened again. Her fingers were stiff, the knuckles white. 'It will do you no good to threaten me,' she said — again very slowly and carefully.

I couldn't stand it any longer. I strode towards her and snatched the receiver.

'Liza . . . Liza, is that you?'

There was no reply. I heard only a breath that might have been a subdued, rustling laugh. Then there was a final click, and silence.

I put the phone down and went and sat beside Ingrid. She put out both her hands and looked at them. There was not a tremor. She hardly seemed aware of me.

'What did she say?' I demanded.

'She intends to enjoy herself,' said Ingrid in an undertone.

'What did she say to you?'

'She told me . . . ' Ingrid paused, as though reassembling fragments of a conversation already forgotten, or translating from another language. ''I shall be watching,' she said. That was the way she put it. 'You are going to be very afraid of me before I've finished,' she told me. 'It will go on for a long time, until you will wish you were dead.''

She spoke almost dreamily. It all seemed

more and more absurdly melodramatic. But then I remembered Liza's hard, bitter face and the rasp in her voice, and I remembered last night's incident. However cheap and melodramatic it might be, it was real.

'She's insane,' I said.

'I am afraid so. I think' — it was incredible how calmly she said it — 'my life will be in danger soon.'

'If she tries anything again — '

'But not yet,' said Ingrid. 'That's not the plan. To frighten me first — that's the idea. To keep me frightened, never knowing what is going to happen next. She told me . . . ' She hesitated.

'You'd better tell me.'

'There are things . . . things I didn't say before. When Liza came to see me . . . '

'I knew there was more!' I cried. 'You didn't tell me the whole story.'

'I was anxious not to worry you. And I didn't take her seriously then. She threatened a lot more than I told you. She said she wouldn't leave me alone. She said . . . '

'Go on,' I urged.

'She said I would have no peace with you. I would never know what she planned to do until it was done. I would never know when she was merely trying to frighten me, and when she really meant to go through with something.'

'Why didn't you tell me this? Why didn't you tell the police?'

Ingrid shrugged. The tautness I had seen in her during that brief telephone conversation had drained away. I couldn't share her tranquillity.

'That inspector was right,' she said. 'His man will never be able to guess what is likely to happen — or when or where. I am the one who will have to be ready for it, to deal with it when it comes. You will have to leave it to me.'

'But — '

'I am in no real danger,' she said. 'She does not mean to kill me — yet.'

Her smile was frightening — set, humourless and feline. She was like one who had accepted a challenge and proposed to go through with it for as long as she could cope.

And how long would that be?

9

It was a relief, that following Sunday, to get out of London.

We were playing a Sunday evening concert at a Manchester cinema, and I decided to leave early in the day. Ingrid and I would go up in my car; the band would follow later in the coach. The coach would bring the boys back overnight, as usual, but Ingrid and I would stay in Manchester on Sunday night and drive back on Monday.

I notified Manton that he could call his watchdog off for those two days. I would be with Ingrid all the time, and I would ensure that we had hotel rooms close together. For a moment I suspected he was going to snicker, but he took it all as coolly as ever.

It was a bright, cold day. Before starting, I gave the car a thorough inspection. My nerves were on edge. I was ready to find that the steering had been tampered with or a tyre slashed. But there was no sign of any damage. We wove our way through the streets of London, and then picked up speed when we were clear at last.

I felt less jittery. Settled behind the wheel, I relaxed. Ingrid was beside me, her lips slightly parted. The road hissed away beneath us. This was how it should be — Ingrid and I in a car together, away from troubles and complications. For several stretches I was able to open up, and we sped away from the tangle of London, where driving and living were both jerky and unsatisfying.

Ingrid pulled her coat up around her ears, and above the purr of the engine I heard her humming to herself.

'All right?' I said.

She smiled. 'Fine.'

Church bells were ringing as we drove through a small town. Their last echoes were drowned by a convoy of thundering lorries; then the traffic thinned out again, and the sun shone through the dark, brittle branches of the hedges.

We stopped at a pub for a drink and

cheese rolls. Sitting in the window, Ingrid looked out at the car. Then she looked down at her dress, and touched it as though to make sure it was real. She was pleased; you could see that it was a moment of acute consciousness — perhaps contrasting what she now had and now was with past unhappiness. I felt a surge of longing for her. I wanted to make her happy and keep her that way. I would find out what her life had been like, and coax her to talk it all out, and then make up to her for it. She was still locking things away inside herself.

We said nothing about Liza all day. The sense of danger had been left behind in London.

I set a fairly leisurely pace in the afternoon. We reached Manchester as it was getting dark, and booked in at the hotel. Ingrid's room was next to mine. I made a point of searching it before letting her enter, but I was not really alarmed. If Liza intended further trouble she would surely wait for us to get back to London.

We went round to the cinema at the time the coach was expected, and when the instruments had been unloaded and carried on to the stage, Freddie and I made a brief check on lighting and acoustics.

There were posters everywhere: THE MELLOW MUSIC OF MIKE MERRIMAN, with THE COOL VOICE OF INGRID LEE.

I had arranged with the hotel to fix us a light meal before we started. The boys in the band swarmed through the building, in that search for lavatories which is so inevitable after a long coach journey.

'I will go upstairs for a moment,' said Ingrid. 'I'll join you in the dining-room.'

'I'm coming up with you,' I said.

'But darling, there is no danger here. You've looked round my room already. Nothing is going to happen.'

I felt that way myself, but I wasn't going to take even the smallest of chances.

'Just the same,' I said, 'I'm coming up with you. And I'll wait in my room until you're ready to come down.'

She smiled. 'I think you're wonderful.'

We went to the desk. I asked for our keys. The receptionist handed over mine, but Ingrid's hook was blank.

'I must have left it in the door when I came down,' she said. 'Yes — I know I didn't hand it in.'

We went upstairs to the first floor. Three of the band passed us, coming down, and the lift doors were closing on the first floor as we went along the corridor.

The key was in Ingrid's door all right, where she had left it. She put her hand on the knob, but I closed my hand over it.

'Let me go first.'

'Mike, dear, you're so masterful!'

She stood aside as I opened the door and went in. Nobody fired a gun at me, or threw vitriol, or hit me with a blunt instrument. I felt a bit silly. This wariness was just what Liza probably wanted to inculcate: she wanted us both to have the permanent jitters.

I said: 'Oh well . . . All clear.'

Ingrid was already coming in behind me. I felt rather than saw her tense, and then she walked casually towards the tiny dressing-table and turned, smiling. But she was not casual enough; and the smile was that disquietingly feline one.

'What is it?' I said sharply.

'There's nothing, darling. No mines exploding under your feet. But thank you, all the same. It does me good to have you as a bodyguard.'

She stood in front of the dressing-table, as still as though she were singing one of her special songs.

I said: 'What have you seen? What are you trying to hide?'

'Darling . . . '

'Move out of the way.' I went towards her, and took hold of her shoulders, and tried to force her sideways. She resisted for a moment, then gave way.

There was a photograph lying on the dressing-table. She must have seen it as she came into the room.

'I didn't want to worry you,' she said.

I picked the photograph up. It was a very clear picture of a pair of hands resting palms downwards on a table. They were hideously twisted, malformed hands. They looked as though they had been ripped open and then stitched clumsily together, with great weals following the lines of the stitches. I had seen such a photograph once before, though not quite as bad as this one. I stared for a moment, then remembered: it had been a picture of a hand mutilated at Hiroshima. But this was far worse.

I said: 'I don't understand. What does it mean?'

Ingrid took the photograph from me and studied it. 'It's impossible to guess what she has in mind,' she said. 'Maybe it is a warning — that she is going to do something to me like this.'

'But how did she get it here? It wasn't in the room when we arrived.'

'No. It was not.'

I caught her arm and drew her with me, out of the room. I took the key with me and we hurried downstairs.

The receptionist blinked as I leaned across the desk and rapped out: 'Has anyone — a woman — been here during the past hour or so asking for Miss Lee?'

'No, sir.'

'You're sure? You've been here all the time: there hasn't been anyone else on duty?'

'No, sir.'

'You haven't seen a woman going in and out?'

He began to frown. 'Is there something wrong, sir?'

I was certainly not prepared to tell him the full story, or even a part of it. All I could say was: 'Is there a woman staying in the hotel who looks not unlike Miss Lee? She'd probably have booked in a day or two ago.'

He looked at Ingrid and shook his head. He was beginning to get on his dignity. 'There is nobody like that here, sir. There are two married ladies here with their husbands, but they are the only two. If you have some particular complaint to make . . . '

'Never mind,' I said.

We went away from the desk and back upstairs.

I tried to recall who had passed us when we last came up here only a few minutes ago. And who had been getting into that lift just as we reached the first floor?

Then I realized the significance of what I was thinking.

I said: 'Maybe this isn't Liza herself.

She may have a collaborator in the band.'

'I had thought of that.'

'But who?'

Ingrid shook her head wearily. 'You know them better than I do.'

'They've all been wandering around. Any one of them could have seen the key in the door.'

'And if there had been no key,' she took me up, 'he would probably just have pushed the picture under the door.'

'It's incredible. For anyone to risk his job — and risk more than that, if we catch him — just because of Liza . . . ' It didn't make sense. 'She and Freddie were always pretty thick,' I recalled, 'but I can't see him doing a damn-fool thing like that.'

I saw her once more into her room, then went into my own and had a wash. I changed into my white band suit, and waited for Ingrid to tap on the wall. Then we went down for the meal.

As we went into the dining-room I instinctively moved closer to Ingrid. I had a sudden vision of a door closing on her fingers, or of something falling and trapping her.

I looked round the faces of the band. I knew them all; I had spent enough time looking at them, goodness knows. Now I was in search of something different. Was there any tell-tale sign that would give one of them away?

I said: 'Where's Cy?'

Cy Mitchell was missing.

'He said he had to dash back to the coach,' said Freddie. 'He dropped his wallet on the floor, and he was a bit worried about it.'

'When did he go?'

'Five minutes ago. It's not far, boss.'

'He could have waited until we went round to the cinema for the show.'

Freddie regarded me curiously.

Ingrid said: 'Shall we start? We haven't a lot of time.'

Would Cy Mitchell come back? I remembered his moodiness — his ups and downs, the way he played badly one night and brilliantly the next. An unstable character. I didn't have any memory of his talking a lot to Liza, or being one of her special buddies; but then, there had been those weeks while I had been away in the States, and there was no telling what had happened then. Maybe he had done this job for her — this pointless job of planting a repellent photograph — and then beat it.

'Anything wrong, boss?' asked Freddie as we tackled the cold meat and salad.

I leaned towards him. 'Are you happy with Mitchell?'

'When he's good,' said Freddie, 'he's very, very good.'

'But not very dependable.'

'He's only had a couple of off nights — and we all have those. He's pretty highly strung, but we'd lose a lot of tone out of the sax section if we didn't have him.'

'He was all right while I was away?'

I waited for Freddie to show, by some twitch of the eyelids or a hesitation in his speech, that he was worried about what lay behind my questions. But he simply looked puzzled. 'Same as usual,' he said. 'I had no complaints, anyway. What's all this about, boss?'

I didn't know what it was about, and Cy Mitchell came back at that moment.

He must have been hurrying; his brow was gleaming with perspiration, and he was breathing hard.

I said: 'Did you find it?'

He sank into a chair. 'Yes, thanks. It had slipped under a seat.'

The rest of them were aware that there was something wrong. I could hardly start cross-questioning Mitchell with them all listening and wondering.

Ingrid was eating the meal calmly enough, but I was unable to finish. I pushed the plate away. Why had Mitchell rushed away? If he had been the one who had planted that photograph, he would have done better to hang about with the others instead of drawing attention to himself by disappearing.

There was no reason to suspect him more than anyone else. Anyone in this room could have been responsible.

'Pass the water down, will you?'

It was Mitchell. Clyde Goff picked up the water jug at our end of the table and passed it to his neighbour. Then he cried shrilly: 'What's hit you, Cy? You've already drunk all your own water.'

Mitchell's forehead was still wet. He seized the jug greedily, filled his tumbler, and drained it in a couple of gulps.

'That dash I had to make to the coach,' he muttered.

I saw that Ingrid was watching him. He prodded at the food on his plate and appeared to wince, as though even the sight of it was too much for him.

Freddie began to discuss the stage on which we would be playing. Had I realized that we would get a rather thin sound from being strung out along it, instead of being built up in the usual formation? Yes, I had realized it. Should we keep Ingrid at the side for her numbers instead of making her walk across the restricted space at the front of the stage? I thought so.

And I looked again at Cy Mitchell.

He was leaning forward, propped against the table. He was still breathing heavily. He might just have sprinted into the room and collapsed. His mouth worked, and he clutched his stomach. Then he caught my eyes on him and forced himself to sit upright.

I said: 'Is there anything wrong?'

'I'll . . . be all right, boss. Just a touch of the gripes.'

But it was all he could do to sit still. Abruptly he pushed his plate away, much more forcefully than I had done.

Fear welled up in me. I forgot the doubts I had had about him a few minutes ago. Something else was stronger; something that made me turn to Ingrid and say:

'Is that food all right?'

Her eyes widened. 'It is good, yes. You should finish yours.'

Cy Mitchell bent forward again.

I said: 'For God's sake . . . If this food is poisoned . . . '

I got up. Freddie hauled his great bulk out of his chair and bobbed up alongside me.

'Poisoned?' he echoed. 'Nobody's dropped dead yet.'

'Don't talk like that!'

'You're a bit keyed-up, boss. This is only Manchester, you know. We're not going to lay any eggs here. All we have to do is play the stuff we usually play, and go home. What's all this about poisoning?'

I looked down at Ingrid. She looked perfectly all right. Then I went down the table to where Mitchell was squirming in his chair.

He said: 'It's O.K. Not to worry. Just a touch of stomach cramps. I get them from time to time. I ought to have brought some medicine with me. I'll be all right.'

'The food,' I said. 'Did you taste — '

'It's not the food,' he said. He wiped his hand across his forehead, and it came away glistening. 'I'll be O.K.'

'You can't play like this.'

I was aware of Ingrid beside me. She had her bag with her and was opening it. She was studying Mitchell's face, as though every line of it meant something to her. A doctor might have looked as she did, assessing symptoms.

She said: 'Here — do you think this might help?'

She was holding out a small black box, the size of a pillbox. Mitchell half got out of his chair, reaching for it. Then he subsided.

'What is it?' he growled.

'I just happened to have it,' said Ingrid. 'You'll find it'll work.'

He took it from her. His face was working. He stared up at her. You would have said that he hated her rather than felt grateful towards her. It must have been pain tugging at the corners of his mouth.

'Thanks, Miss Lee,' he said at last.

She nodded and turned away.

Freddie was beginning to fidget. 'Time we got going,' he said. As Ingrid and I moved past him, he hopped back and bumped into a chair.

Other chairs scraped back. We got our coats and went out. Cy Mitchell had gone off to the lavatory. When he came back he was still damp and exhausted-looking, but he could stand upright.

'Better?' I said.

'Getting a lot better, thanks,' he said.

I was still not happy about the food. Had a plate been switched? Something meant for Ingrid might have got to Mitchell by mistake.

But there was no way of finding out now. And it couldn't have been very

143

serious; he looked better every minute, and by the time we got to the cinema he was beginning to laugh and hum a chorus with the tenor player.

He played beautifully that evening. The whole band was in form. I knew it — but I couldn't enjoy it. Facing them, I was conscious of the audience massed at my back. When Ingrid was on I tingled with a sense of exposure. Liza could be out there in that audience — watching, enjoying herself. I ought to have stood at the doors and watched them come in. I ought to have done *something*.

Nothing happened. But if Liza had wanted anything to happen I couldn't have stopped it.

10

During the next fortnight there were several incidents. Taken on its own, each might have been regarded as little more than childishly spiteful — or even as an accident. It was the cumulative effect that counted. It was unnerving not to know when Ingrid was being attacked and when she wasn't. That car that swooped alongside the pavement, its lights blazing through the rain, splashing her with filthy water from the gutter — was that part of the campaign, or was it a normal London hazard? The torch that was suddenly flashed in her face one dark night, and then flicked away, vanishing along with a faint laugh before I could pursue — that, surely, was deliberate?

The plain clothes man on watch was not much use. As Manton had said, there was no way of guessing when and where Liza would strike. There wasn't even a fool-proof way of ensuring that she didn't somehow get into Ingrid's block of flats: people were coming and going the whole time, and without a large-scale police cordon there was no way of checking them all.

I wondered, once or twice, whether Ingrid was hiding anything from me. She could be receiving telephone calls without admitting it. Often she looked pale and apprehensive, but she always denied that she was getting any threatening calls. When I suggested that we ask the police to tap her phone, she refused. Nevertheless, I felt that I might have a word with Manton. There might be a way of arranging it, and then Liza could be tracked down during the course of a call. I was sure there were such calls and that Ingrid just didn't want to worry me. I'd sooner have had everything out in the open; I was worried enough as it was.

One evening there was quite a crowd as we approached the Tivoli. Some girls recognized us and came milling around, blocking the entrance to the stage-door alley. I signed a couple of autograph albums, Ingrid signed some, and we eased our way through. As the crowd at last parted, something was thrown on to the pavement at Ingrid's feet. She stopped. I moved quickly in front of her and picked it up.

It was a surgeon's scalpel.

I straightened up and tried to look over the heads of the girls who were drifting away. The neon lights and the jostling people made it hard to pick out any one figure. Perhaps that dark, slightly hunched shadow disappearing round the corner . . . but I didn't stand a chance of reaching her.

I took Ingrid's arm and we went towards the door. Inside, I said:

'What do you suppose this means?'

She took the scalpel from me and turned it in her hand. Light gleamed down it.

She gave an uncertain little laugh. 'It must mean that she wants to cut my heart out — literally.'

I said: 'Ingrid, there . . . there isn't anything that you're not telling me, is there?'

'What could there be?'

'It all seems so pointless at the

moment. It doesn't add up to anything. If there were some clue to — well, to what's behind it all . . . ' I floundered. After all, one did not expect logic from a woman who had apparently gone mad.

The next day, when I called for Ingrid, I noticed a torn envelope in her waste-paper basket. One edge was turned back. I recognized the writing. I had known it for long enough.

Ingrid came into the room. I said: 'You've had a letter from Liza.'

She opened her mouth as though to deny it and set my mind at rest. Then her eyes followed the direction of my gaze.

'You're too observant,' she said softly.

'You weren't going to tell me,' I accused her.

'No.'

'What was in the letter? Where is it?'

'I have burnt it.'

'But why? You should have kept it. It ought to have been handed over to the police.'

Ingrid shook her head.

'Why didn't you keep it?' I persisted. 'At least you ought to have shown it to

148

me. It might have given us a lead.'

'It was . . . too foul,' she said. 'More threats — put in such a terrible way. It would only have hurt you.'

I bent down and took out the three fragments of envelope, hoping the postmark would yield at any rate some guidance. The corner was crumpled, though, and the postmark itself was heavily blurred. There was nothing to be gained there.

I said: 'If you get any more like this you're to keep them. Do you understand? Ingrid, you must promise not to try and hide things like this from me.'

I waited.

'I promise,' she said.

The next night she was late coming on the stand ready for her opening number. She ought to have been below us, waiting, before we went into the opening bars of the introduction. I prolonged the break between numbers for as long as I could, and then leaned over the piano towards Freddie.

'Take them through a slow foxtrot,' I said. 'First chorus piano and rhythm, while the rest of them sort out the parts.'

I slipped down into the corridor and went along towards Ingrid's dressing-room. There were two girls outside, just turning away from the door. One of them saw me, and squealed at me.

'Mr. Merriman, we can't get in.'

I felt cold — terribly cold. Then I was there, rattling the handle of the door.

'Ingrid.'

'Mike,' she said from inside.

'Let me in.'

'I can't. I've been locked in. I can't get out.'

There was no key in the outside of the door. I glanced along the corridor. Wherever it was, it had not been thrown down here.

I said to one of the girls: 'Go and get Sandy out of his box at the door. Tell him we want a key for this room.'

She stalked away, the feathers on her bottom swaying like those of an ostrich. Maybe they were ostrich feathers.

I got close to the door. 'Are you all right?'

'Yes, I'm all right . . . now.'

'There's nobody else in there with you?'

'No. I was afraid . . . when I found the door was shut . . . '

There was a silence that seemed to last for ever.

'Sandy's bringing a key,' I said.

He came at last. He opened the door, and I went in. Ingrid was standing in the middle of the room. She swayed as I went towards her. But all she said was: 'We're late. I must go on.'

'Take it easy,' I said. 'You don't have to go on right away.'

'It'll do me good.' She was already on her way out of the door. In the corridor she took my arm. 'I was a fool. I was so scared for a moment. Locked in there — and I thought there might be somebody in the cupboard, or behind the curtain . . . '

'You're not going out there to sing. You've got to rest.'

'Where would I rest? Not back in my dressing-room. And I don't want to go home. I just want to go out and sing. It's better that way.'

She did not falter. She sang, and there was no tremor in her voice. If anything, it was harder than usual: the way she threw out the lyrics sounded bitter and contemptuous, and there was a roar of applause when she had finished. She was truly wonderful. I knew that, although I was only half listening. The rest of my attention was focused on the problem of who had locked her in and taken the key away, or thrown it away. At the end of Ingrid's first set of numbers I went to see Sandy and asked if a woman had come in. He was prepared to swear that no one but the regular cast had come through. Certainly Liza had not appeared. He would have spotted her at once. Something in his manner told me that he would have been glad to see her. A lot of people were fond of Liza. He couldn't see any connection between a locked door — 'Bit of silly mischief, if you ask me' — and Liza.

Someone in the band then? There had been a brief interval before we started that particular sequence, and several of them had been off the stand. I couldn't remember who they had been, though.

On the Sunday morning I got up early — I had not been sleeping well since this damnable business started — and telephoned Ingrid. She answered the phone at once. Was there a tinge of apprehension in her voice? 'Oh . . . Mike,' she said with a faint sigh when she heard me.

'I didn't wake you up?' I said.

'No. I've been awake for ages.'

I suggested we went for a walk. It was a clear, cold, crisp morning. We drove up to Hampstead Heath and walked across, coming back to the car in a long ellipse. Ingrid hardly spoke, but the sharp air tinged her cheeks with a flush that made her look young and carefree. That was how I wanted her to be.

We drove into Highgate and had a drink, then back to Knightsbridge for lunch. It ought to have been a happy morning, but we had little to say to one another. Behind anything casual we tried to say there was always the menace of the thing about which we simply could not be casual.

We went to the cinema in the late afternoon, and had dinner together. When

I took her home I insisted that she ring me first thing in the morning. I wanted to be sure; I had to check on her every day. From now on I would begin the morning with this telephone call. I wondered why I hadn't decided on such a system before. A late night kiss, when I took her home from the Tivoli, and the sound of her voice in the morning . . . and between those times, the assurance that she was at home and wouldn't answer the door on any pretext whatever.

There was no joy, now, in being with her or in leading the band that had once meant so much to me. There wasn't even any joy in anticipation; until Liza was found we couldn't make plans of any kind.

On Monday evening I was called to the telephone just before the Tivoli show started.

'That you, Mike?'

It was Dave Blair.

I said: 'How are you getting on, Dave?'

'That's what I was going to ask *you*. You haven't been in to the Club for a long time.'

'Life's been pretty hectic.'

'Yes. Since Liza went away.' He sounded accusing. I didn't reply. After a pause he went on: 'Why don't you drop in tonight for an hour or so? Bring a couple of the boys along if they'd like to sit in on a session of real music.'

'I'll ask them if anyone wants to come,' I said. 'But I think you'd better count me out.'

'I'd like to see you.'

'Some other time, Dave.'

He persisted: 'I want to talk to you.'

'You're talking to me.'

'I'd sooner we could sit down somewhere and have a drink.'

'Look, Dave, we haven't got much to say to one another.'

He said: 'I've had a message from Liza.'

I made him repeat that. And he added: 'I talked to her on the phone.'

'Tell me,' I said.

'Not like this,' he said. 'I hate telephones. Words don't mean anything over the phone. Come round and see me.'

I said: 'If you're in this filthy game with Liza — '

'What the hell are you talking about?'

'You really don't know?'

'Come and sit where I can see you,' said Dave. 'Then I'll know whether you're as crazy as you sound.'

'I'll come after the show tonight,' I said. 'And I'll bring Ingrid.'

'I don't know that that's a good idea.'

'I'm bringing her,' I said.

I went to the band. During the first interval, with Ingrid beside me, I said:

'Anybody want to do some jamming in The Chord Club?'

Freddie shrugged. He was too fat and too lazy to do any extra-mural work if he could help it. Sitting in with an improvisatory group had never been Freddie's idea of fun. Cy Mitchell looked at me half-enquiringly, as though debating whether to spend another hour or two of wakefulness with his mouth wrapped round his alto mouthpiece. I didn't encourage him. An alto was fine in my own set-up, but it wouldn't go too happily in Dave's little group. A tenor was much more welcome. I glanced at Warren, who was a very versatile character: he could produce a throb that gave a quite individual tone to my sax section, but he was also capable of blowing hard, angular choruses that made him sound like a sort of Bud Freeman of the nineteen-fifties.

He lifted a wispy grey eyebrow. 'Dave Blair's lot?' he said. 'Nice. Wouldn't mind. Could let my hair down.'

'Both of them?' said Clyde Goff, leering out between his cymbals.

Jack Winter said he would be prepared to carry his trombone round to The Chord Club.

When we had settled this, and I had gone down from the platform with Ingrid for a drink, she said:

'Why are we going to this Club?'

'Dave Blair invited us,' I said.

'We haven't been before.'

'He's heard from Liza,' I said.

'So.' She breathed the word between her teeth.

'He sounds cagey about it,' I said, 'but if he's got anything to say when we meet, I very much want to hear it.'

The main trouble with The Chord Club was that it brought Liza back so vividly. I could almost believe that she was here — not somehow on the other side of the room, skulking and awaiting her chance, but right here beside me. The band was going strong on *I Know That You Know* as we came in, and it was all so familiar and so reminiscent.

There wasn't a table to spare. Even on Mondays, it seemed, Dave could pull the faithful ones in. We leaned against a wall until the number was finished, and then he saw us and came across.

'I'll fix you up,' he said. 'Here — you boys take your horns on the stand, and grab a couple of chairs. What'll you have to drink? Here, I can shove these two characters into the corner; they're used to it. Right. Make yourselves at home.'

I said: 'Dave, I don't think you've met Ingrid, have you?'

'No.'

They shook hands. Dave didn't look as though he enjoyed the experience.

The band kicked off on a fast blues. Without Dave's lead trumpet they produced a low register, tight growling sound. It was infectious. It made a lot of people want to get out on the little floor and dance, and at the same time they wanted to listen to what was going to happen.

Drinks appeared in front of us.

Dave didn't lead up to it gently. He just said: 'I'd like a word with you alone some time, Mike.'

'You can say anything you like right now,' I said.

He looked with frank distaste at Ingrid and then back at me. 'No,' he said. 'When I say alone, I mean alone. That's why I invited you here.'

I began to get up. 'If it's like that, Dave — '

'Sit down and don't be so bloody stuffy,' he said.

Ingrid said: 'Darling, it's all right. I'll go and powder my nose. Or wash my hands.'

'Facilities aren't all they might be in this dump,' said Dave, with only the faintest apologetic tinge in his voice.

'All right,' said Ingrid. 'When the band finish that tune, I'll go and sing with them. Then you boys can let your hair down.'

'They won't know your sort of number.'

'I'll sing one of the old ones,' she said. 'I do know some of them — I've been educated, you know.'

'By all means,' said Dave.

We pushed our chairs round so that we were all facing the band. A three-sided conversation wasn't possible — not between we three.

Funny. In spite of everything, I found that I was enjoying the music. I'd had no sort of kick out of my own stuff for weeks, yet here I was sitting back and enjoying the outmoded choruses these boys were pounding out. The atmosphere of The Chord had something to do with it. It was an atmosphere made up of smoke and memories. Nostalgia for the simple life, I thought scornfully. But still I went on listening. I was with Dave's pianist as he took over from the trombone and went into a solid, rocking chorus. Nothing showy. No large, harsh spread chords. A nice inventive line, with a left hand that kept driving along. Two choruses. Three. And then the low, exciting growl of the front line as they took over and riffed their way to the end.

Dave turned and looked at me enquiringly.

'Good clean fun,' I said.

Ingrid got up. The inevitable heads turned as she went towards the band.

Dave said: 'My God, she's beautiful.' He didn't sound at all approving.

There was a brief pause while Ingrid and the band went into a huddle. I wiped my eyes. They were stinging with smoke.

'What did Liza say to you?' I demanded.

He put his elbows on the table. His hair stood up above his forehead as though twisted back by some ferocious draught.

He said: 'She asked me for news of you.'

'That's nice.'

'It doesn't mean a thing to you, does it?'

'It means a hell of a lot,' I burst out. 'After Liza's behaviour these last few weeks — '

'What are you talking about? She's been away.'

I told him. While I was talking, the

band started. Warren breathed a first slow chorus of *Melancholy Baby* into his tenor. I was halfway through the story when Ingrid began to sing. Automatically we turned towards her. Dave's thick, bruised trumpeter's lips pursed as he watched. He looked incredulous — not at her singing, I felt, so much as at the thought of her being persecuted by Liza.

Ingrid didn't belong in this cellar. You knew it the moment she opened her mouth. Her style was all wrong. The notes were there, the words were there, and the ice-cold delivery was the same as ever; but it didn't match up with the accompaniment the band was playing. This *Melancholy Baby* sounded as though it had been left out for the night on the bare mountain.

The pianist took over for a reflective chorus, and I went on and finished the story of Ingrid and Liza.

And Dave said: 'I never heard anything so fantastic. You can't believe that?'

'You don't think we dreamt it all, do you?' I shot back.

He stared at Ingrid again, as she leaned

against the piano, waiting for the last sixteen bars to come up. He shook his head.

'I don't know what that woman's done to you,' he said, 'but if you're capable of believing that Liza would ever be mixed up in that sort of lunacy . . . '

I reminded him about the threats Liza had made when she called on Ingrid.

'You've only got her word for that,' he said, nodding angrily towards Ingrid.

'What about the envelope — in Liza's handwriting?'

'Did you see the letter itself?'

'No, but — '

'If I were you,' said Dave with bitter deliberation, 'I'd check on the past history of your new woman, and see what skeletons are rattling about there.'

Ingrid was taking up the last half-chorus. I leaned across the table and said: 'What did Liza say to you on the phone?'

'I told you I hated telephones. Things don't mean what they ought to mean, often enough. But even over a telephone I can tell you that Liza was still in love with you.'

'Enough to assault anyone who was likely to take me away from her?'

'That's not Liza,' he said. 'She's moved out of your life. She's left you to it. All she wanted to do was check up and see if you were happy. Poor kid — she was really asking me whether there was any hope; whether you were tired yet; whether she stood any chance at all. And I got the impression that if she were quite sure you were happy, and that you were absolutely finished with her, she'd come back and let you have your divorce.'

I didn't feel like laughing, but I laughed. I said: 'Tell her to come back then.'

'I'd like to bash your face in,' said Dave. 'If it weren't that I want this club to stay open, without any disorderly business, I'd bust your nose open right now.'

'The perfect host,' I said.

The number was ending. There was a spattering of applause. This wasn't the Tivoli by a long way.

Dave glanced round. Ingrid was talking to his pianist. She would be back with us in a moment, unless they decided to do another number, and the mood of the place was against another one.

He said: 'I can't tell her anything, because I don't know where she is. Maybe she'll ring me again. Maybe she won't. I told her I'd ask you along here and we'd have a talk. She didn't want me to do that — said it was no good. Looks as though she was right. Poor kid.'

'Poor kid,' I echoed derisively. 'With her threatening letters and vitriol bottle and — '

'And her big car splashing your precious mistress with water . . . '

'Ingrid's not my mistress,' I said.

He stared. Then he snorted. 'God, man, aren't you getting *anything* out of this? I wish I'd been able to tell Liza that.'

He stood up. Ingrid was on her way back. I saw a man at a nearby table lean back over his chair and let his hand droop so that her bare arm would brush against it as she passed.

She reached us and said: 'Am I too early?'

'We've got nothing further to say to one another,' said Dave thickly. 'Nothing at all.'

He began to edge round his chair.

'Wait a minute,' I said.

'Anything you have here tonight is on the house,' he said. 'But don't come back again, Mike.'

Ingrid watched him go. 'Well,' she said faintly. 'We should not have come here.'

'You're right. For all the good it's done . . .'

'What did Liza say to him?'

I told her. It was little enough. Oddly, I sensed that she was relieved. Had she been expecting another barrage of threats, relayed this time through somebody else? I reached across the table and took her hand.

'Shall we go?'

'Please.'

We got up. Dave led the band into *Someday Sweetheart*, making no attempt to come and say goodbye or even wave to us. That was all right by me.

I held the door open for Ingrid. You pretty well had to slide out into the small space at the foot of the steps. The only light outside was a garish yellow bulb beside the door.

166

Ingrid had her foot on the bottom step. I half turned to pull the door shut. And then there was a crack and the splintering of glass. The light went out. For a moment, before our eyes could get used to it, there was near darkness down here.

In that moment I heard the scuttle of feet down the steps. Ingrid screamed, and screamed again.

I tried to get past her. There was hardly room, the steps were so narrow. I was aware of her falling back against the wall with her hands up to her face, sobbing in great gasps. Then I sprang over her legs and went up the steps. A shadow obscured the light at the top and was gone. I came out into the street. The shadow wasn't there. In this shabby quarter there were too many side streets and alleys. It was hopeless.

And down there, still huddled up, was Ingrid.

I plunged back towards her. I got my arm round her shoulders and tried to help her up. She was a dead weight. She refused to take her hands away from her face.

'Darling' — I couldn't keep my voice steady and reassuring — 'what is it? What happened?'

With one foot I kicked the door, and it opened. I led Ingrid inside, back into the smoke and dusky lights. Across the room Dave looked at us and stopped playing.

Ingrid leaned against me. She took her hands away.

A woman at the nearest table screamed.

Ingrid's cheeks had been swiftly and expertly slashed with a razor. The skin had been neatly turned back to reveal a red rawness that seemed to burn in the twilight of the cellar.

She sagged and collapsed.

Dave Blair was with me now, taking part of her weight. I stared at him across her slumped head. I was shouting.

'Poor kid!' I yelled. 'Poor kid, you said. You told her you'd asked us here — and this is the result!'

11

They turned the flaps of skin back up and put stitches in. They treated her for shock. I stayed with her until she was asleep, and next morning — or, rather, later that same morning — I telephoned the hospital. They said she was sleeping, but would be able to see me in the afternoon.

When I arrived, Ingrid was sitting up in bed. I could hardly bring myself to look at the hideous, inflamed pattern on her cheeks.

'Darling, I'm all right,' she said, as though I were the one in need of protection against pain and fear. 'They say I must stay here tonight, and then tomorrow I can come out.'

I had been thinking things over on the way here. I said: 'I'm not so sure. Maybe you'd be safer if you stayed in hospital for a while.'

'No.' It came out sharp and instinctive. 'I . . . I hate hospitals.'

She was still upset. It was hardly to be wondered at. I tried to soothe her. 'You can rest here and take things easy, out of harm's way, while the police really get down to some work. I've already raised a stink with Manton — '

'No,' she cried. 'I won't stay. They say I can get up and go, and that is what I shall do. It . . . it could be easier for her here. So many things are possible in a hospital.'

I didn't want her to get too excited. But I said: 'You can't go back to your flat. If you come out, you come and live with me. I want you with me.'

'I was with you last night, and it didn't stop her.' Then she reached out to me. 'No, my darling, I don't mean it that way. I mean that we can never know when she will strike, or how. Being together isn't much help — in a practical way, that is. But in the other way . . . ' Her fingers tightened. 'I need you,' she said very quietly. 'I will come and live with you.'

I collected her the next morning and took her home with me. Here she could rest until it was time to go back and have the stitches taken out. I would spend every moment of my free time with her. And when I was at the Tivoli, or broadcasting or recording, I would make sure there was some adequate guard on her.

After lunch that day I made coffee and Ingrid lay on the divan. Just as I took the cups away, Manton arrived with a burly, cherubic-faced man.

'I've called the Yard in on this,' Manton explained.

'About time,' I said.

'I've told Chief Inspector Lake the whole story, but he'll probably want you to go over it again, filling in all the details.'

That was exactly what Chief Inspector Lake did want. He settled himself on my smallest chair, threatening to overflow its edges — rather like Freddie, I thought incongruously, without any piano in front of him — and asked me to put him in the picture.

I went right through the thing from the beginning. He made no comment. Then he asked Ingrid a few questions to clarify certain points. They were shrewd questions. His baby face was deceptive.

When we had finished he said: 'I don't

believe a word of it.'

Fury boiled up inside me. 'If you'd gone through what — '

'Hold it, Mr. Merriman. Hold it. I'm not casting doubt on your word.'

'What *are* you casting doubt on, then?'

'The whole set-up is utterly impossible,' he said. 'I've no doubt all these things have happened, just as you've described them. But they simply can't mean what you think they mean.'

'What other theories can you trot out?' I asked sourly.

He put his hands on his knees and wriggled round on the chair to face Ingrid. He might have been studying a corpse for all the human warmth there was in his scrutiny.

He said: 'That work on your face has been done by an expert. It's very neat. An amateur can never do a razor job like that. People who run amuck with a razor tend to hack and cut — you get a few dangerous gashes, and you can lose an eye. But that slicing business — and done in the dark, at that — is the work of a professional.'

I couldn't stand it; I was about to

interrupt when he fired the question at Ingrid: 'Who in the underworld has got a grudge against you, Miss Lee?'

'Nobody,' she said with a dignity that ought to have put him to shame. 'Nobody that I know of.'

He swung back to me. 'Is your wife the sort of woman who would engage a crook to do a job like that for her?'

'I'm willing to believe anything about her now,' I said.

He pouted. You would almost have expected him to blow bubbles. Manton glanced at him with a mixture of respect and unease. When he spoke, his usually sceptical voice sounded strangely mellow and affable after Lake's perturbing blandness.

Manton said: 'We'll find out whether your wife is behind it, or whether it's all on a different plane altogether. In the meantime . . . ' He waited to see if Lake wanted to speak. Lake was silent. 'Where,' asked Manton, 'are you living now, Miss Lee?'

'She's going to stay here with me,' I said, 'where I can keep an eye on her.'

'Like you did the night before last?' said Lake mildly.

Manton hurried on. 'You'd be a lot better off in hospital, miss,' he said. 'In the circumstances, we could probably arrange it.'

'No,' said Ingrid.

'But — '

'I couldn't bear to stay in hospital. It is one of those things that . . . no, I must be out. I shall be safe here.'

'If you would only agree to stay in hospital, out of harm's way, until we had settled this matter . . . '

'No,' said Ingrid.

I said: 'It comes to something when someone's got to be virtually imprisoned before you can guarantee them protection from anyone who happens to be going around with a grudge against them.'

Lake wriggled. 'We have a hard job, Mr. Merriman,' he said — not very apologetically. 'We just do the best we can. I'll arrange for a permanent guard in this building — right outside this flat, in that little hall you've got. There'll be comment, of course. Publicity. This has gone too far now for that to be avoided. We'll make an announcement, too — really go all out to get Mrs. Merriman in and question her, just to satisfy you.'

'To satisfy *me*?' I said.

'And ourselves,' he conceded wryly.

'There have already been God knows how many pictures in the papers,' I pointed out. 'What difference is a new appeal going to make? Unless you're going to accuse her outright of being a criminal — which you seem reluctant to believe.'

'There's a way of wording it,' said Manton. 'You've seen it before. The police would like to interview Mrs. Liza Merriman, who it is believed may be able to help them in connection with an investigation into the slashing of Miss Ingrid Lee at The Chord Club . . . '

'All right,' I said. 'All right.'

Manton said: 'Can I use your phone? I'll get a man to come here before we leave.'

He made the call, and then they waited. Lake heaved himself upright and plodded round the flat, testing the windows and studying the approach to the small hall from the staircase. Manton took a chair out and set it beside the lift. I made some more coffee.

A plain clothes man arrived. After a brief consultation with Manton he moved the chair to a different position. Sitting in it, he could command the staircase and the lift, and there was no way of getting past him unobserved.

I showed him how he could get into the lavatory immediately inside my front door, and gave him my spare key. There was no need for Ingrid to have one: she was not in any circumstances to go out of the flat on her own.

Lake and Manton prepared to go.

At the door Lake swung round. 'We'll get to the bottom of this, Mr. Merriman,' he said with a sudden disconcerting false heartiness. 'Don't you worry — we'll find the truth of it.'

He wasn't even looking at me. He was staring past me at Ingrid.

Lake and Manton hadn't just left a guard behind. They had left an atmosphere as well. Ingrid and I didn't have much to say to one another. I caught myself glancing at her from time to time, and each time she seemed to be expecting it. Once she gave me the faint ghost of a smile and shook her head, and I felt ashamed without knowing why.

I tried to sound cheerful. 'That character Lake isn't the brightest boy I've ever met.'

'He doesn't appear to like me,' said Ingrid.

'That's one of the things I meant. Still I suppose the police distrust everything and everybody.'

'I suppose so.'

When I left her, after boring the man on guard with my demands for assurance that he would not move from the spot until I was back from the Tivoli, I was guiltily glad to get away. I longed for them to find Liza and pull her in. Only when Liza had been found could we begin to live. This unnatural existence, with the constant fear nagging away through every minute and hour, was freezing something inside me. And Ingrid — would she suddenly crack; would she be frightened away, frightened into leaving me and not coming back?

I wanted her so much. Yet because of all this I could not be happy when I was with her.

There was quite a crowd at the Tivoli that evening. News had been travelling. A lot of them came to gloat: I could feel them staring at my back as I conducted, as though expecting that the sight of it would reveal something the newspapers hadn't hinted at. Bloodshed was evidently not bad for business. Scandal didn't keep the people away.

It made me sick. Now that I was away from Ingrid I wanted to be back with her.

One of the floor show girls did a couple of solo numbers to fill in Ingrid's solo spots. She was all right. They liked her. She had obviously been waiting for a chance like this; it was the sort of chance from which many a career has been fashioned.

The crowds, I thought, would swarm in the night Ingrid came back. I could just imagine it.

Somehow we reached the end of the

show. I was out of the building before Les had emptied the spit out of his trumpet. Now I was wildly impatient to get back.

The guard was still there, waiting to be relieved by a colleague. There was, in fact, five minutes to go. I waited until I had seen the new man come on duty, then let myself into the flat.

I moved quietly. If Ingrid had gone to sleep I didn't want to disturb her. But I had to look into her room to see if she was all right — I had to hear the sound of her breathing and know that nothing unforeseen, nothing hideous had happened.

Cautiously I opened the door. The darkness was impenetrable. For a moment I was sure that the room was empty . . . empty of life, anyway.

Then Ingrid said: 'Is that you, darling?'

She sounded very wide awake. And as I hesitated in the doorway she switched the bedside lamp on.

'Everything all right?' I asked.

'I've been waiting for you,' she said.

The light must have dazzled her. She raised one arm to cover her eyes, and the sheet fell partly back. She was naked.

I had told myself that I wasn't going to make love to her. I wasn't going to try. She had come here to be looked after, and nothing was going to happen — not now, not until she was better, not until everything was cleared up the way we wanted it to be. But it just had to happen.

She lay in my arms and repeated: 'I've been waiting for you.'

The marks on her face were dark and angry, but she did not try to hide them from me. She offered me the beauty of her body in defiance of what had been done to her face. And as I clung to her, and in one moment of ecstasy looked into that face, I found her studying me with wide, questioning eyes. She looked almost amused. It was a trick of the light. That was what it must have been — a queer shadow in the corners of her eyes.

She did not move. She lay still. She was receptive — no more.

And I was not the first.

She knew I had realized it. She said: 'Darling, you can tell . . . '

'Yes,' I said; 'I can tell.'

'Is it too important?'

'No,' I said.

Yet it was. The icy purity, the untouchable mystery of her . . . I had wanted to be the first to despoil it. I was wretched. And I was wretched not because of Ingrid and the knowledge that there had been another man — maybe more than one — in her past, but because of the sudden realization of my own selfishness — the ugliness, even, of my own desires.

She murmured: 'You can forgive me?'

'My dearest,' I said, 'there's no question of forgiveness. I haven't asked what you did before I met you.'

'I will tell you,' she said, 'one day. And you'll forgive me?'

'Of course.'

'Anything?'

'Anything,' I said.

12

And then there came the telephone calls.

The first, next morning, was from Dave Blair. I didn't want to hear anything from Dave Blair. I was on the point of replacing the receiver when I recognized his voice, but he said swiftly:

'Listen to me. I want you to get one thing straight. This attack on Ingrid — it's foul, and I've had nothing to do with it. Not even by accident.'

'Leave it,' I said. 'It doesn't do any good now. The thing's happened.'

'I wasn't the one who told Liza you'd be at my place that evening,' he persisted. 'How could I have done? She spoke to me only the once, and then I didn't know which night you'd be coming along — even if I could get you to come at all. She was all against the idea of me inviting you, anyway. And I didn't know Ingrid was going to be with you: that wasn't in my mind at all, even when I was actually inviting you to come. So rule me out, will you?'

'All right, Dave,' I said. 'All right. I'm sorry.'

'Never mind,' he said. 'No apologies. No arguments. It's all mad, anyway, from start to finish. This crap in the papers this morning . . . '

He left it at that and rang off.

Then there were calls from several papers. Two reporters came round to see me and to ask where Ingrid Lee had disappeared to. When they saw the man sitting outside the door, doubtless they began to put two and two together. They were able to produce stories for their papers which were full of hints that weren't hints at all — just informative enough to tell anyone who wanted to know where Ingrid was just where she in fact was.

I waited, now, for Liza to attack again. Or to write. Or to telephone.

Houses at the Tivoli stayed good. Saturday night was even more noisy and crowded than usual. The crowd would have preferred Ingrid to be there, but in her absence they still seemed to enjoy having a good look at me and passing dirty jokes around beneath the cover of the music.

Sunday we lay in bed until noon. The Sunday papers had revived some details of the story, right the way back to its beginning when Liza disappeared. I skimmed through them, then tossed them aside. All over Britain, this morning, millions of men and women were lying in bed or yawning at the breakfast table as they read about Mike Merriman and his two women. A rewarding thought? Good publicity? Like hell.

Just as I was thinking it was about time to haul myself out of bed, the phone rang.

The bedroom extension was on Ingrid's side of the bed. She picked up the receiver immediately, as though she had been waiting. I saw the lines in her face tighten; whiteness ran along the angry edges of her scars. Without a word I snatched the phone from her.

This time I did not snap out a challenge. I just listened.

What I heard was baffling. I had been

so sure it would be Liza's voice that the sound was quite alien for a few seconds — unnerving in its lack of meaning. Then I pulled myself together and said: 'I'm sorry, but you must have a wrong number.'

There was silence. Then came a whisper of something disturbing, a whisper like the laugh I had thought I heard once before. Then it was gone. The line went dead.

Ingrid's head had fallen back on her pillow. She turned towards me.

I said: 'It sounded like German. Not that I know any German.'

'Darling, you snatched it out of my hand before I could even say 'Wrong number',' protested Ingrid. She smiled gravely. 'We are both . . . jumpy.'

That night we lay in one another's arms again, and still she was cool and unroused. Her body was exquisite under my hands, but there was one awful moment when, like a tantalizing demon, the memory flickered in my mind of Liza and how she had always responded: I remembered her warmth and abandon

— and suppressed the memory quickly, with something amounting to panic.

No. I must be patient. I loved Ingrid. She was all I had now. This love of ours had got to prove right. When she was well, when the fear and uncertainty of this interminable waiting time had gone, she would be happy.

On the Tuesday morning the phone rang while I was in the bathroom. I came out to find her replacing the receiver.

'What was it?'

I shot the demand at her almost like an accusation.

'A wrong number again,' she said.

'In German?' I asked.

She hesitated for a fraction of a second, then said: 'It must have been German, yes. The woman must have trouble with the English dialling.'

I took her that afternoon to have the stitches removed. There was a dour, sandy-haired man in the front of the car, and a police car followed unobtrusively at a reasonable distance.

The marks on Ingrid's cheeks now looked like a neat ridge of bruised flesh, puckered and drawn inwards. They told her it would all heal — in time. Heavy make-up would hide the worst of it for the next few months.

I thought of that damaged face exposed to the harsh spotlights and the glare of the audience.

We drove home. We had not been indoors for more than ten minutes when the phone rang. We looked at one another. Ingrid lifted one hand, then let it fall. She might have been trying to summon up the courage to lift the receiver — or to command it to stop.

I crossed the room and picked up the receiver.

This time the voice was Liza's.

13

Liza said: 'Mike, what do all these newspaper stories mean?'

'I think you know,' I said. 'If you don't, who does?'

If only I had fixed for the police to tap this phone! I stared at Ingrid across it and jerked my head towards the door. She frowned slightly and didn't move. I didn't dare to cover the mouthpiece for a moment and tell her to get the man outside.

'This is crazy,' Liza was saying. 'I've been out of touch — away from newspapers and everything. I've only just seen all this stuff. I rang Dave, and he told me that you really have some mad idea that I've been attacking Ingrid. It isn't true, is it?'

'Isn't it?'

I tried to indicate, by making faces at her, that Ingrid should warn the guard. Still she did not understand. She simply looked at the telephone receiver in my hand as though it might bite.

Liza said: 'I just don't begin to understand. Mike, I've got to talk to you.'

'Keep talking,' I said.

'Not like this,' she said. 'I want to see you. Can you meet me somewhere?'

It was too good to be true. There must be a catch in it somewhere. I said: 'Where are you right now?'

'I'm at Paddington. I've just got in. I could see you in about twenty minutes at . . . well, what about the little place in Marylebone High Street where we used to have coffee? Remember?'

'I remember.'

'You'll play fair, won't you?' she said abruptly. 'I don't know what this is all about — this police appeal, and all the rest of it — but I don't want to have the police brought in yet. Not until we've talked. No police — no fuss.'

'All right,' I agreed.

'I can trust you,' she said.

'Yes.'

'In twenty minutes then.'

'Twenty minutes,' I said.

Ingrid waited for me to speak. I sat

189

down. Then I got up again, and began to pace up and down the room.

I told her what Liza had said. And I said: 'What do you suppose she's up to? Discounting the pleas of innocence, what do you think she hopes to achieve by seeing me?'

'I don't like it,' whispered Ingrid.

'Maybe she thinks she can start to dictate terms now. But why didn't she do that over the phone?'

'It is a trick,' said Ingrid with sudden fervour. She held her hands out to me. I took them, and looked down the smooth whiteness of her arms. 'She wants to get you away from the flat,' she went on. 'She will not be at the place you have arranged to meet. Once you are out of the way, she will come in.'

'She can't get past the man on duty,' I pointed out.

'She is clever. She must have some plan.'

I said: 'I think she's on the level. She wants to parley. I know Liza. There was something about the way she spoke . . .'

'You still have a high opinion of her,'

said Ingrid tonelessly.

'It's not that. It's just that . . . '

But I could not finish. I could not explain just what it was about the well-remembered sound of Liza's voice that made me so sure she had been in earnest when she made that appointment.

'You are going, then?' said Ingrid.

'Yes,' I said, 'I'm going. I'm convinced she'll be there. And if she's there, you can't possibly be in danger here, can you?'

⋆ ⋆ ⋆

Liza was already there when I arrived. I didn't realize this for a moment. I peered in through the windows, through the mass of indoor plants which had been trained up a trellis immediately inside the little restaurant — and there was nobody there that I recognized. But when I went in, and looked at a table in the far corner, I saw her.

It gave me a shock. No wonder there had been no success in attempts to trace her. She wore a drab little hat — what you could only call a sensible hat — and beneath it her hair was neat but not in the least like Liza's glossy, tightly-drawn hair had always been. Instead of the sort of tight, sleek coat she had invariably worn, she now leaned back in the corner in a loose, casual brown coat. It made her look shapeless and uncaring. And it made me think, at once, of that cloak effect, swirling round the running figure, the menacing shadow . . .

The lights were so coyly shaded that everyone sat in half-darkness. I slid into the chair opposite Liza.

'Hello, Mike,' she said. 'How are you?'

She sounded as though she really wanted to know.

I said: 'A large black coffee, as usual?'

'What a memory you have!' Now there was a touch of bitterness, and that made me feel a lot better.

I ordered two black coffees, and then said: 'Well? What do you want to say?'

She propped her elbows on the flimsy table. I marvelled again at the change in her. There was no resemblance to Ingrid now. I realized just how much Liza had been my creation — Liza the Sex Chill, that is, as opposed to this woman who sat before me. She was . . . well, the only way to put it was that she was mature, womanly — and ordinary. Nicely ordinary. Comforting.

Only I didn't derive much comfort from her.

'I want you to do the talking,' she said. 'I want you to explain everything that's been going on while I've been away.'

'Look, Liza, don't let's play round with it. You know and I know that you've been behind it . . . '

I stopped as the waitress came and put the cups down in front of us. When she had gone away Liza said:

'I wouldn't even know what you were talking about if it weren't for what Dave Blair told me over the phone. Until I saw that police handout I had no idea I was suspected of anything. And what Dave told me just sounds like the craziest fantasy. Mike . . . please . . . won't you give me the whole story?'

'I'm wasting my time,' I said. 'I came here because I thought you had something to say — an ultimatum, or something.

But this is getting us nowhere.'

She cupped her hands round her coffee cup. It was an old habit. She looked cold. But there was nothing cold in her eyes or her voice. She demanded:

'Mike — *tell me!*'

And because of something in her that I remembered from what seemed a long time ago, and something that made me very uneasy, I said: 'All right. So you didn't threaten Ingrid with a bottle of vitriol?'

'Good heavens! No.'

'Or telephone her?'

'No.'

'Or write to her?'

'No.'

I wanted to shatter that terribly convincing certainty of hers. I said: 'But I happen to have seen the envelope of the letter. I recognized your handwriting at once.'

Liza shook her head in apparent bewilderment. 'I've never written to Ingrid in my life. I . . . Wait a moment. Yes. I wrote to her once, about some dress fitting. It was early on, when she first came into the Tivoli show. Long before the two of you went on the American tour.'

'And you think she'd have kept that envelope specially in order to get it out and lay it in her waste-paper basket where it would catch my eye?' I said derisively.

'Some people have envelopes hanging round for a long time. And as to deliberately putting it where it would catch your eye . . . well, I don't know. Perhaps you're closer than you think, Mike. Because something very queer is certainly going on — and if I'm not involved in it, then your precious Ingrid Lee has been telling some tall tales, by the sound of it. And I can assure you I'm not involved. So?'

'You didn't go to see her before you went away?' I fired at her.

This time I scored a hit. She flushed, and lowered her eyes. Reluctantly she said: 'Yes. I went to see her. That was how desperate I was, Mike. Desperate enough to think that maybe, just before I walked out, I could have a last attempt. I knew you were blinded by your infatuation. I thought Ingrid might, after all, be a reasonable human being I could talk to. I appealed to her. It hurt me — by God, it hurt me, Mike. But I wanted everything suddenly to be all right, and I went to her, and . . . well, it showed me that things couldn't be set right as quickly as that.'

'You threatened her.'

'Threatened her?' Liza's wild laugh made a muttering couple at a nearby table turn round and study us warily. She lowered her voice. 'I hadn't got any weapons to threaten her with. I slunk away with as much dignity as I could muster — and it wasn't much — and went off into the country. I didn't look at newspapers, I didn't listen to the radio. It was only by chance that I saw this new appeal for me to come forward. And here I am, Mike. But I want nothing to do with the police.'

'I can imagine that,' I said.

Our coffee was getting cold. Liza sipped at her cup, then sat back.

She said: 'You really think I'm mixed up in this cheap shocker that you've concocted. Or' — she put out her right hand accusingly — 'is that what you're doing: is this just a gag to get me to show myself, so that you can do something about divorce proceedings?'

'And you didn't slash Ingrid with a razor,' I snapped back at her, 'or hire someone to do it?'

'Oh, Mike!' Something seemed to crack. There were tears in her eyes. She had never cried easily, and my instinctive reaction was to go and put my arm round her and tell her to take it easy. But the tears could be — surely were — just another symptom of her present instability. 'Mike, what's happened to you? Maybe you've fallen for somebody else, but how you can believe . . . I never thought . . . '

'Ingrid recognized you,' I said, 'with the bottle of vitriol. You spoke to her. You threatened her over the phone, too. And — '

'Ingrid told you this?'

'She'd hardly have made it up just for the fun of it.' I said.

There was a pause. Liza got control of

herself. She stared obstinately down into her coffee, not wiping her eyes, letting the tears dry. Then she said carefully:

'I walked out and left no address because I didn't want to give you a divorce. I knew if I'd stayed I'd have weakened. You would have talked me into it, just as you talked me into so many other things. What I thought was that if I just disappeared, and left you and Ingrid to sort it out between you, you'd soon realize what kind of woman she was. I've got my pride, you know, Mike. I don't think you realize quite how much. I wasn't going to go down on my knees and beg you to stay with me. If you'd kept on at me I'd have given in and made what arrangements you wanted to make. But if I were just not there — if you had a chance of seeing what a cold bitch you'd picked for yourself . . . then I thought there might be a chance. I had my pride, all right — but I would have come back to you, Mike, once I knew you'd got over the silliness.'

'So you went off into the country to meditate?' I said.

'I had my reasons.'

'Someone like you, living in the entertainment world all that time, eating and sleeping and breathing in the city — you mean to tell me you just went off for a quiet spell in the country?'

'I had my reasons,' she repeated.

'Away from it all!' I mocked her. 'Listening to the birds in the trees — when we thought you were trying to frighten Ingrid into keeping away from me! Which sounds the most likely possibility to you?'

Liza said: 'I'd advise you, Mike, to find out more about Ingrid's past. There must be a lot of things in it that she doesn't want you to find out. If she says she recognized me as a vitriol thrower, she's lying. If she says I telephoned her, she's lying. I haven't written to her. I haven't attacked her.'

'What possible reason — '

'That's what you'd better find out. And quickly. There must be something she daren't tell you. Whatever these crazy threats and attacks are, she's using me as the one to blame simply because she daren't let you into the truth. She's playing for time. That *must* be it. There can't be any other explanation.'

'That's all you've got to say?'

Liza sighed. She looked very tired. 'Yes, that's all.' Then she forced the words out: 'You're still in love with her?'

I recalled the disturbing amusement in Ingrid's eyes, and the coldness of her in my arms. Then I blotted out the memory. I said: 'Of course.'

'In that case, I might as well give up.'

'Give up? You're admitting, then — '

'I mean,' she said, 'that you can have your divorce. I've been wasting my time, hoping you would see sense. Evidently you're still blind. All right, Mike. I give in.'

There seemed to be nothing to say. You didn't say 'Thanks very much' in such circumstances. And I didn't want to exasperate her into further excesses by asking outright for her promise that the attacks on Ingrid would cease.

Liza suddenly added: 'I'm going away again now. I'll send you my address.'

'You can give it to me now.'

'I'll send it to you,' she said very firmly,

'when I read in the papers that you, or the police, or anyone in the world, has cleared up the matter of the attacks on Ingrid. I don't propose to become involved in any questionings myself. I just want to be left alone — a long way from here, where it's peaceful and I can do things the way I know they've got to be done.'

'This is ridiculous,' I said. Did she imagine she could just walk out like that, scot-free? 'You can give me your address here and now.'

'You'll get it,' she said, 'and you can start divorce proceedings — we'll fix it any way you want it — when the truth has been established. That is' — her smile had its old, arrogant sneer — 'if you still want a divorce then.'

This was enough. I stood up, and pushed my right hand three times down the back of my head, smoothing my hair. Liza stayed where she was. She said:

'I'll wait here for a few minutes, Mike. You run along. Obviously we haven't got any more to say to one another, have we?'

I heard the door swish open and shut behind me. Footsteps came across the room. I saw Liza's face as she looked past me.

'I see,' she said. 'Even your promise that you wouldn't tell them you were meeting me — that didn't mean a thing, Mike?'

'Not when I was dealing with someone as dangerous as you,' I said.

There were two women, with Manton behind them. They were pleasant, fresh-featured women, and one of them had a genuinely friendly smile; but they were watchful, and their healthy appearance owed a lot to the tough training they had had.

'Mrs. Merriman?' said Manton quietly. Liza nodded.

'Let's move off, shall we?'

It was carried out very decorously. The couple who had been surreptitiously watching Liza and myself may have had some inkling of what was going on, but nobody else appeared to realize. I paid the bill and we went out. A block down the road the police car was parked by the kerb.

Manton said: 'We can go straight to the

station and have a little chat.'

'I've got a better idea,' I said. 'Let's go round to my place.'

'No.' Liza swung towards me so violently that one of the policewomen shot out a restraining arm. 'I won't. I refuse to go there.'

'We might as well carry out the enquiry in civilized surroundings,' I said.

And then I stopped. As Liza was urged gently towards the car I saw why she was wearing a loose, voluminous coat. One of the policewomen noticed, too, and asked her something quietly and affably.

And if her story about wanting to go away into the country and stay there had been true, here was a plausible reason.

I said: 'Liza — why didn't you say something?'

'About what?'

'You're expecting a child,' I said.

'Eventually. Months to go yet.'

'But you didn't say — you didn't tell . . . '

'I told you I had my pride.'

'But . . . '

She got into the back of the police car,

with one of the women on each side of her. Manton and I squeezed in the front with the driver.

I was overpoweringly conscious of her there, behind me. She was so silent. I wanted to twist round in my seat and question her — but suddenly I realized that I knew the answer. I remembered. There had been that night just before I went to America — giving her the jade earrings and making love to her. Love. I had been half in love with Ingrid already. A great wave of shame washed over me. I remembered Liza's warm, desperate response then. Yes, I remembered the desperation.

Angry, fighting down these thoughts that did no good, I said: 'Go to my place. We don't have to sit in one of those dismal rooms at the police station.'

'It's customary to go to the station,' Manton demurred.

'I don't want to be taken to the flat,' said Liza from behind. 'Please — no.'

'Why do you sound so worried about it?' I demanded.

'You've got no sensibilities at all, have you?'

Manton said, with unexpected brutality: 'Are you afraid of meeting Miss Lee?'

I said: 'That's it! We can confront Mrs. Merriman with Miss Lee.'

'Or the other way round,' said Liza in a remote, dead tone.

Manton muttered to the driver.

When we reached the block of flats the driver waited outside. The small lift was meant to hold four people, but the five of us wedged ourselves in it. I tried to look searchingly into Liza's face; she stared back with an expression that was not even one of hatred — it had gone beyond that.

The lift sighed to a halt. Through the gates I could see the chair outside my door. It was empty.

Manton swore. 'Where's the damned man got to?'

'Probably in the lavatory,' I said.

I fumbled for my key and opened the front door.

'It's all right,' I called out.

There was no reply.

I stood there for a second, then tried the lavatory door. It was open. I pushed, and it stuck against something.

The man was there all right. He had been battered behind the right ear with the bronze figure of a negro dancer that had stood on the corner cupboard in the sitting-room. Blood was black down the side of his face.

I didn't wait to see if he was still alive. With Manton at my heels I went on into the sitting-room.

'Ingrid . . .'

She was there. She lay sprawled across the couch with her head back, her face turned away. I sobbed as I rushed towards her. And still, after all this time, I can feel inside my head the sound that I made when I saw her face.

She had been strangled.

14

It seemed to take no time at all before the flat was full of people. Flashbulbs exploded. There was always a burly man answering the telephone or making urgent calls on it. The two policewomen sat in chairs on each side of Liza, who was very pale; for some reason they looked protective rather than imprisoning.

I felt sick. But my legs wouldn't push me out of my chair and across the room.

The police surgeon had been bending over the man who had been on duty here. When he stood up he drew a long hissing breath through his teeth.

'Looks like a nasty concussion. Lucky to be alive. We'll have to get him down as gently as we can. Ambulance here?'

'Came a couple of minutes ago, sir.'

'Good.'

They moved the man. Still there were too many people in the place.

Lake arrived. He was unshaven. His baby face looked ridiculous with its dark fuzz of bristle.

He came right to me and said accusingly: 'Well?'

'What sort of a guard do you call that?' I burst out. 'As soon as I go out, he lets himself get beaten up. And . . . and . . . '

I was going to break down if I said any more. I had to hold on to myself.

Lake swung towards Manton. 'How did it happen?'

Manton told him the story tersely — what there was of it.

I slumped back while they talked, and across the room my eyes met Liza's.

She said: 'How are you going to twist this one, Mike? I suppose you'll accuse me of luring you away so that . . . so that . . . '

She had to stop. She, too, was close to the edge.

Lake heard her. He nodded, and pushed his fat lower lip out towards me. 'Do you still accuse your wife, Mr. Merriman?'

'I don't know,' I said.

The room was beginning to expand. Then it contracted. Their faces crowded in on me. I tried to blink them into focus. It was all dreamlike.

Somebody in the background said: 'O.K. You can take it away now.'

They removed Ingrid's body. I stared at the floor, watching it blur and recede, until I knew she was gone.

Ingrid: gone.

'Now,' said Lake.

He was plodding round the room with his hands behind his back. He peered at the bookcase, at a pile of music in the corner, at the couch, and then at me. He was blaming me for the whole business.

I hit back. I said: 'Why did your man let the murderer through?'

'That's a question I'd like to ask him. It may have to wait. He's concussed. May be able to talk sense in an hour or two; may take days. In the meantime' — his perambulations brought him to Liza — 'what can *you* tell us, Mrs. Merriman?'

'I know nothing about it,' she said.

'Why did you draw your husband away from the flat this afternoon?'

She told him what she had told me. Only this time she mentioned the child she was expecting. My child. And she said: 'I had my pride. I wasn't going to fog the issue with any appeal to him on those lines. I didn't want him to know. I wanted to stay away and have the baby, and say nothing about it until I knew he wanted to come back to me. To *me*.'

I knew Liza. Sitting there and watching her and listening to her, I realized just how well I knew her. She was telling the truth. To me there just wasn't any doubt about it. And my mind rocked at the thought of what that meant.

'You didn't arrange this appointment with Mr. Merriman,' said Lake, 'in order to give an accomplice time to kill Miss Lee?'

For a moment it appeared that Liza did not consider this worthy of a reply. Then, wearily, she said: 'No.'

Lake resumed his prowling. Then he stopped close to the armchair which was pushed against the telephone table. He seemed to hover over it. Slowly he lowered himself and plucked a small book from the side of the cushion.

'What's this — anything special?'

I recognized it at once. 'Only my address book,' I said. 'Addresses and phone numbers — agents, music publishers, members of the band and so on.'

'No significance at all?'

'No,' I said. Then I said: 'Wait a minute.'

'Well?'

'What's it doing there?' I asked.

'Where do you usually keep it?'

'In the pocket of my grey overcoat. I usually transfer it to my raincoat if I'm wearing that, but today I went out in a hurry.'

'There's no reason why it should be here? You haven't used it today and just put it down on the table? It could easily have been knocked off there into the chair.'

'I haven't used it.' I was sure of that. 'But Ingrid knew where I kept it. If she'd wanted to ring anyone — '

'While you were out?'

Liza said abruptly: 'I fancy she would be very anxious to ring someone.

Whatever game she was playing, she must have known it was nearly up: if my husband was really going to meet me, there was a danger I'd be able to persuade him that all her stories about being attacked and threatened by me were lies.' She grimaced wryly. 'I'd be inclined to say it wasn't much of a danger — he was not convinced — but she wasn't to know that.'

'But her accomplices, if she had any, wouldn't be in my address book,' I protested. 'And in any case, you can't claim she deliberately let herself be slashed the way she was just in order to pull off some weird scheme she had?'

Lake thumbed through the book. It evidently offered him no inspiration. I didn't see how it could.

'If only Jefferson would come round,' said Manton despondently. 'If only he could tell us why he let anyone past him — '

As though in answer to his plea, the telephone began to ring. Lake snatched it up.

'Yes?' His eyes switched towards me.

'What's your name? What do you want him for?' There was a pause, then he held out the receiver to me. 'Says his name's Freddie. Wants to know if anything has happened.'

Manton laughed mirthlessly.

I said: 'Freddie? Mike here.'

'Boss, what's the idea? We should be starting any minute now. Has anything happened to Ingrid?'

I told him what had happened to Ingrid. And while he was still making incoherent noises at the other end of the line I told him that he would have to carry on without me. It all carried a hideously reminiscent echo of an earlier conversation — of Lew's call when Liza disappeared. But Liza had come back. Ingrid would never come back.

'O.K.?' I said at last.

'All right, boss. We'll do our best. We're one man short, though. Cy Mitchell hasn't turned up.'

'Cy Mitchell?'

'I'll ring his place — I've got his number somewhere — and see if he's there. Maybe he's got held up on the way.'

Lake was watching me all the time I talked. Something in his perpetual, unrelenting suspiciousness communicated itself to me. I said to Freddie: 'If you don't get any reply, ring me back. At once.'

'Sure, boss, but — '

'At once,' I repeated.

I waited. Lake asked no questions. When the phone rang again, I answered, and he went on watching me with fat, monumental patience.

There had been no reply from Mitchell.

'Well?' said Lake.

'A member of the band hasn't shown up. Once or twice he's acted queerly.' I sketched in the incident on our Sunday night provincial session, and when I put it into words it sounded pretty shallow. 'But I don't see what it adds up to,' I finished lamely.

'His address?' said Lake.

I nodded towards the address book. He opened it, found Mitchell's address, and reached for the phone. Life was held together by the phone. It nagged, ordered, threatened — and when you wanted to start things moving in the outside world you found that it governed all that, too.

Right at this moment the band would be starting to play in the Tivoli. Playing without me. None of it had anything to do with me any more. Things had become too violent for music and shuffling dancers to mean what they used to mean. Reality was not in the Tivoli: it was not Ingrid, sleek and beautiful, singing into a microphone; it was a corpse that had been removed, and a fat man who was snapping commands into a phone.

Liza said: 'I'm very tired. Do you need me any more?'

Lake bobbed round towards her as though about to launch some accusation. Then he pushed his hands into his pockets and wagged his head. 'Where are you staying in London, Mrs. Merriman?'

'I'm not staying in London. I'm living in Wales — a long way away from this sort of thing.'

'If you're tired,' he said, 'you won't want to go back there tonight. And we'd like you to hang around for a day or two.

This investigation is only just starting. Let us find you a hotel — '

'Am I being charged with anything?' said Liza flatly.

Lake raised an eyebrow. He raised it at me.

Manton, putting it into words, said: 'Are you preferring any charges against your wife, Mr. Merriman?'

'How can I?' I said.

Liza's smile was sad. 'Is that the best you can do, Mike?'

She looked washed out, sitting between those two confounded women. It was monstrous that she should be there.

I said: 'I believe that my wife has told you a true story. For some reason, Miss Lee's reports of attacks on her and threats made against her were all false. I think that she took advantage of the situation to lay the blame for what was happening on to my wife. I think she was involved in something she didn't want me to know about.'

'I think so, too,' said Lake.

'But you still want me to stay in London?' said Liza.

'It would be a help to us. There are going to be so many ends to tie up. If we get a chance of going through every one of Miss Lee's specific accusations and checking the lot against any other facts that come to light, we may be grateful for your assistance. Certainly we ought to talk tomorrow, when you've got over the shock of what has happened here.'

I cleared my throat. With difficulty I said: 'Liza . . . You don't have to go to a hotel.'

She flinched. 'You're not suggesting . . . '

'I'll sleep on the divan bed,' I said. 'You can get a good night's sleep here, and tomorrow we can see the inspector and answer any questions he's got. It will save everyone a lot of trouble.'

Liza turned to Lake. 'If I have to stay in London,' she said, 'perhaps you'll do as you suggested, and find me a hotel.'

'We'll do that,' he said.

He made no immediate move to follow this up, however. The prowling mood seized him again. He paced up and down, his head on one side. He might have been trying to sense something from the very atmosphere of the room.

After a few minutes he said: 'What was Miss Lee's background, Mr. Merriman?'

'She came from somewhere in the north,' I said. 'She never really said where.'

'Do you usually employ people who cannot give details of their homes or previous employment?'

'In the entertainment business,' I said, 'you employ people for what they are. In this case we were quite happy to leave the background mysterious: it was all part of the publicity build-up.'

'For the general public, all right,' he conceded. 'But wasn't she more explicit with you?'

'I always felt' — it sounded pitiful now — 'that sooner or later, when we . . . when everything was settled, and we got round to talking freely, she'd tell me. When she was ready.'

Once more the phone jangled into life. Another message from the world. Another link, a clue, a fragment of truth or a misleading voice.

Lake said: 'Yes. Lake here.' His eyes glazed over as he listened. His right thumb started an odd little movement, counting the fingers of his right hand. 'I'll be right round,' he said at last.

He put the receiver down and looked at me.

'Cy Mitchell was at home,' he said. 'He hadn't left for the Tivoli. He couldn't. He's dead. Shot. Looks like suicide.' His lower lip came out in a way I was beginning to know too well. 'What do you suppose he and Miss Lee meant to one another, Mr. Merriman? You never noticed anything?'

I had seen Ingrid dead, and seen her face. Somehow I had taken it all in without going down. But now, all at once, I had had enough. I couldn't take any more. The room went out of focus again, and this time it dissolved into darkness.

15

There came a moment when I struggled up out of oblivion and wondered where I was. Then I turned over and felt the coolness of the pillow against my cheek. I was in bed. There was silence. It was the stillness that I recognized as belonging to the very early morning, without even the undertone of traffic throbbing four blocks away.

I tried to force myself into wakefulness. There was a lot to think about. There were questions that needed answering.

But it was no good. Warm fingers wrapped themselves around my mind and pulled it down again. I muttered something, and I had an idea that a minute or two later somebody opened the bedroom door and looked in. Then I was gone again.

When I finally awoke it was morning. I rolled over and looked at the clock beside my bed. Nearly eight-thirty.

There was a smell of coffee.

I rolled out of bed. My legs felt heavy, and I had to make a conscious effort to force my hands to get hold of my dressing-gown and pull it on. It was like a hangover, only made up more of a drugged sleepiness than of drunkenness.

I went out and into the sitting-room.

Liza was at the table in the window, eating toast and marmalade.

It was such a familiar sight that I could almost have believed that I had been dreaming the whole business of Ingrid and the violence and the death of Cy Mitchell. Dreaming: that would account for the heaviness in my limbs and inside my head.

Liza said: 'You should have stayed in bed.'

'What happened? What are you doing . . . ?'

The words slurred.

She said: 'They gave you a sedative. A very efficient one, by the look of you. They said they'd be round to see you this morning — later this morning — with any information they'd acquired. And probably with some questions.'

'But you — ' I tried again: 'What are you doing here? After what you said . . . '

Her face was stony. 'After what I said, I'm a fool. But there was such confusion here. They didn't want to leave you alone, they didn't want to have to spend time finding me somewhere to stay, and they were anxious to go ahead with investigating Mitchell's death. I volunteered to stay with you.'

'Thank you.'

I reached a chair and sat down. She buttered some toast, spread marmalade on it, and pushed the plate across to me.

'It was the practical, sensible thing to do,' she said. 'Drunk, sleepy or doped — I'm used to most of the things you can achieve.'

She poured coffee for me.

I said: 'It's true, then, Mitchell was killed.'

'Mitchell,' she said, 'appears to have committed suicide. Because he had killed Ingrid, maybe? Because of some love affair you didn't know of — or something quite different from that.'

I couldn't concentrate. How had it

come about that my wife and I could be sitting on opposite sides of the breakfast table, talking about two deaths which were somehow tied up with our own lives? What was she doing here — she who had been suspected, for some time, of planning assault and maybe even murder herself?

When the doorbell rang I let Liza answer it. I made myself sit quite still, trying to clear my head. If this was Lake, I wanted to be able to work out what he was talking about. I wanted to have the right questions and the right answers firmly fixed before we started.

It wasn't Lake. It was Lew Simons.

His handshake was as all-embracing as usual, but it had a different quality to it. Instead of being clammily hearty, gripping as though to convey all the goodwill and congratulations and admiration in the world, it was a funeral sort of handshake. He held on to me solemnly, and then said:

'Look, Mike, this is serious.'

Liza came back into the room behind him. He apparently had no comment to make on her reappearance. She slipped back into her chair, while Lew relinquished my hand and stood in the middle of the carpet, shaking his head dolefully.

I said: 'If you mean I'm in the doghouse because I failed to turn up at the Tivoli last night, I must plead pressing problems elsewhere.'

'I know, I know. Look, boy, nobody could feel more dreadful about this affair than I do. But nobody. The trouble is, it's not just one item. Some of the bits of trouble have been good publicity in their way, but there comes a time when the stuff starts to hurt. You got to have an instinct to work out when things start to go wrong. And I'm telling you, Mike: you're getting yourself a bad name.'

Liza gasped; then laughed. Lew turned reproachfully towards her. Things seemed to click into place now. He said: 'You've taken your time about coming back, haven't you, Liza? If you'd shown up before, maybe things wouldn't have worked out the way they did.'

'Leave her alone,' I said.

'Have a cup of coffee,' said Liza.

Lew shook his head. But when she carried a cup of coffee over to him he took it abstractedly and used the spoon to wave at me.

'Let's get down to it, Mike.'

'He's in no state to discuss business now,' said Liza.

'I just want to leave him with a few ideas,' said Lew. 'It's no good leaving it all to make its own way. I mean, the show goes on at the Tivoli every night. Can't just walk out and leave it. Some solid thinking's got to be done — and the sooner the better.'

'Are you telling me,' I asked, 'that they don't want the band there any more?'

'Look, Mike, it's too soon for them to make any decision. This news only broke last night. I got a call late last night because your Freddie had been telling everyone there what had happened, and they wanted to sound me out and see what I knew. When things have cooled down we can see what they think a bit more clearly. But this I can tell you — the reputation of a place like the Tivoli can't stand a lot of dirt. A bit, all right. But it's a family place after all — smart, but not that smart. It might be an idea to take a rest until . . . well, until the inquest and the police stuff and all the rest of it is finished with, and the newspapers have finished tossing your name around. Which is what they'll be doing for some weeks. Anybody been here on the trail this morning?'

'Five or six of them,' said Liza.

I started. 'What?'

'You were still flat out. I told them to get on their way. When they tried to interview *me*, I slammed the door on them. But they'll be back.'

'You're darned right they'll be back,' said Lew. 'Unless I miss my guess there'll be more than one of them hanging about on the corner of the street, waiting for a lead. Anyway, like I was saying, you got to think things out, Mike. What about dissolving the band and retiring for a couple of months? Let the noise blow over, and then form a new outfit. You could do a Continental trip first — easy to fix — then back to a series of concerts all over the country. After that you walk back into a big resident job.'

My first impulse was to argue. I opened my mouth. Lew didn't wait. He said:

'Mike, right now you're no use to anyone. I know this racket. You got to rely on my instinct. I'm putting you wise now, so you can get it all figured out in advance. Don't let the suggestion come from anyone else. Have it all worked out for yourself.'

The arguments simply would not come. I said: 'I can't get interested in the thing. Do you realize two people have died, and you're talking business as though — '

'Sure, I know. Right now it's tough. But I want you to know I'm with you. Right behind you, Mike.'

'Lew,' said Liza, 'will you get out of here and leave him alone?'

Lew took one look at her and went.

There was a silence. I don't ever remember a silence like it in all my life. There had to be some words you could use, but I had no idea what they were.

Liza was calm, but not in the way she used to be. It was not the icy mask that she used to wear — that I had taught her to wear, when building up the character of the Sex Chill. That had been an artificial Liza; this one, I saw, was one I had never known. She had a womanly placidity — yet it was not merely softness, not just a relinquishing of herself.

She was an utter stranger to me. Too much had happened.

I thought again of Ingrid — of Ingrid alive, and Ingrid as I had seen her the evening before — and there was nothing to say.

The doorbell rang again. This time I moved towards the door, but Liza brushed past me.

'Don't get caught,' she said tersely.

I let her go. I heard her speaking crisply to someone, and then the door closed again.

She came back. 'Another reporter. I said you can't talk to anyone.'

Again it rang.

I said: 'It's no use. You can't keep trotting to and from the door. I may as well face them — and tell them to go to hell.'

I went out and opened the door. This

time it was Manton. He was beginning to look very tired.

'Won't keep you a minute,' he said.

He came in, and we sat down. Lake, he explained briefly, was busy and wouldn't be troubling us. He gave the impression that this was purely a routine visit: Lake himself obviously felt that Liza and I now had little to offer. Men were checking on Cy Mitchell and Ingrid.

'Jefferson,' Manton went on, 'has come round.'

I sat up. Liza seemed to stop breathing.

'He's a bit hazy,' said Manton, 'but he's given us the general story. Miss Lee telephoned and asked Mitchell to come to the flat — this flat. She told Jefferson he would be coming, and said it would be all right to admit him.'

'The fool!' I broke in. 'He'd been told — '

'When he's well enough,' said Manton grimly, 'we'll discuss that with him at some length. But his story is that when he objected, Miss Lee said Mitchell was a member of the band, and she wanted him to bring some music round for her to run through, to pass the time. All he was going to do was bring it, settle a few points with her, and then leave. Jefferson argued, but she told him not to be silly. 'It's a woman you've been told to watch out for,' she said. 'This isn't a woman: it's one of the band.''

'Anyway, Mitchell got here. Jefferson let him in, but he was uneasy. He wasn't going to let himself be lured away from his post at the door; but he quietly opened the front door, and tried to listen. For a few minutes they were talking in low voices. Then they began to get excited, and he got the impression they were arguing. He heard a gasp, and then it stopped. There was a scuffle. Jefferson went in. He says he remembers seeing Miss Lee huddled up on the couch, but he didn't know whether she was dead then or whether Mitchell finished her off afterwards. Probably she was dead. Mitchell swung on Jefferson, grabbing the first thing that came to hand. It was that statue. He bashed Jefferson back into the lavatory and battered him on the head.

'Mitchell cleared out after that. He

went home and seems to have started packing. Then he shot himself.'

Liza said: 'Why did he start packing if he intended to shoot himself?'

'That's the sort of thing you often get in cases like this. There are always inconsistencies — because human beings are inconsistent. Mitchell was some sort of manic depressive, up one minute and down the next. Commits a murder, starts to make a getaway, then despairs and kills himself.' Manton was studying me now, the pouches under his eyes yellow and sad. 'There were some pretty obvious features in his behaviour, Mr. Merriman. You didn't notice anything?'

'He was a bit erratic,' I said.

'Yes. When the doc had finished with him he told us the man had been a dope addict. You didn't know that?'

'No,' I muttered.

Yet at once things began to tie up. His varying moods, his wildly inspired playing when he was high, his sweating and cramps on that Sunday trip of ours, and the little black box that Ingrid had handed to him . . .

'You don't suffer much from addicts in your band, Mr. Merriman?'

'Certainly not.'

I had seen some of the troubles that American bands had. In some places the words jazz and dope were almost synonymous. But it had never been rife in England. English musicians got by on pep pills supplied on National Health prescriptions.

Manton said: 'We're trying to find out more about Miss Lee's background. If she was tied up in some organization with Mitchell — or if she was supplying him with the stuff through channels that she controlled . . .'

The little black box, I thought again. But I didn't believe it; whatever Ingrid's background was, I couldn't see her implicated in the dope trade. It didn't fit. More likely that on that one occasion Mitchell had lost his little supply of coke or whatever it was, and Ingrid had picked it up. It might have taken her a little while to realize just what it was.

I was making excuses for her. And all the excuses in the world still didn't explain the accusations she had made against Liza, or why she had called Mitchell round to the flat.

'May I look round the — ah — room she occupied while she was here?' asked Manton quietly. 'We took a lot of stuff away last night, but perhaps if you could point out her personal possessions — any luggage she brought with her — we might find something that would give us a lead.'

I took him into the bedroom, aware of Liza's unwavering stillness.

'Some of the clothes in the wardrobe are hers,' I said. 'There's not much; she didn't transfer all her things here from her own flat.'

'Somebody's round there,' said Manton. 'If you can just point out which were Miss Lee's possessions here, please?'

I indicated the case in the corner. In the wardrobe I remembered which dresses were hers. Liza's were still there: they had not been moved.

'This music case?' said Manton.

'No, that's Liza's.'

He collected what he wanted, and was evidently anxious to be on his way. As he got ready to leave, Liza said:

'Have you any theories at all, Inspector?'

'None we care to commit ourselves to, Mrs. Merriman. But we do think the explanation is going to be a simple one. Something between Miss Lee and Mitchell — some jealousy, maybe, or a blackmail threat, and possibly some unsavoury dealings in the dope-peddling market.'

'But the attacks on her,' I protested: 'how do they fit in?'

'We'll find out,' he said confidently.

When he had gone we were left with that silence again. Liza was the one to break it. She said:

'Poor Ingrid.'

There wasn't anything to say to that.

Then she added: 'Poor me.'

I stared.

'I wanted to wait until you saw through her and came back to me,' she said. 'I wanted to stick it out until you were glad to come back to me. But now Ingrid's gone. She's gone too quickly. You've lost her with one blow, and you've got the torment of knowing that somehow she and Mitchell were tied up together. The police will fill in the details — and it's going to hurt, isn't it, Mike? The clearer it gets, the less you're going to like it.'

'You're not making sense,' I said.

'It's too neat this way,' said Liza. 'It just can't be as tawdry and ordinary, can it, Mike? Not for you it can't. You'll never get over it.'

16

At the inquest, the coroner's jury returned a verdict of murder against Cy Mitchell. And for Mitchell himself, they decided it had been suicide while the balance of his mind had been disturbed. The facts were enough; there was no legal need to dig into motives.

The newspapers, however, did not neglect possible motives for murder and suicide. They had plenty of scope. I was offered a large sum by one Sunday paper for my life story, linked with that of Ingrid. If I didn't want to write it myself, it could be ghosted for me. In fact, they would prefer to ghost it from any brief notes I cared to give them. I refused. Liza was also asked for several instalments of her memoirs; she also refused.

Lew had been right about the band. When I went back the crowds were getting ugly. There were two sorts of people. Some audibly said: 'How he can do it, and her just killed so horribly . . . Standing up there as though he couldn't care less.' Others watched me with a sort of greedy approval. I wondered how I was going to get a permanent replacement for Ingrid. Maybe the time had come for a big change. There would have to be a new gimmick of some sort.

I brought myself up, realizing with horror what I was doing. I was already concocting some new person.

I must quit the band. I would have a rest, wait for the noise to die down, and then start again.

Lake came to see us. It was little more than a rounding-off ceremony.

'We can't find a damn thing about Ingrid Lee,' he admitted. 'Her insurance card came to you, Mr. Merriman, from the coffee bar where you found her. It was blank when she started there — we've checked on that — but it's easy enough to get an insurance card.'

'There's no way of finding out where she came from in the first place?' asked Liza.

'We're continuing our enquiries, on the

chance that she was tied up with some dope ring. We may stumble on something good. More likely not. The soundest idea is that she came from the provinces — up north, probably — in answer to some advertisement. You know the sort of advertisement I mean. Or else maybe she was recruited up there by some pimp — '

'Shut your filthy mouth,' I cried.

He pouted at me. 'That's the sort of background you usually find for someone who seems to have no background at all. Sorry, Mr. Merriman, but we're just fumbling around.'

'Fumbling is right.'

'Anyway,' he said, 'I don't think there's much you can do for us now.'

Liza said: 'You mean I can go now? You don't want me to hang about in London any longer?'

'You can go. And thank you for your patience, Mrs. Merriman.'

He gave her a smile of almost doggy friendliness and shook hands with her. He shook hands with me, too, but not with any fervour. Then he left.

'So that's that,' I said.

I couldn't accept it. It was all as Liza had said — too neat, and too tawdry. Everything had finished, yet there still weren't any really certain answers.

'If my small case is still here,' said Liza, 'I'll pack a few things in that and take it.'

So there was an even deeper, dizzier emptiness below the one I was already experiencing.

I said: 'Liza . . . you can't go back to Wales now. Not after all this.'

'Why not? Nothing has changed.'

I was a coward. I didn't want to let go of her. For so long, in so many different ways, I had relied on her, and now I wanted to clutch her and hang on.

I said: 'I've been a fool. I know it. Liza, I can't sort things out — not here and now — but if you'll be patient . . .'

'Please, Mike.' She was quick and breathless. 'Don't say any more. Just leave it. I'm going.'

'You said you were waiting for me to see reason. I'm seeing reason now.'

'No,' she said. 'Not yet. This isn't the right time. Not yet, Mike.'

She was not to be shaken. When I tried

to touch her she did not flinch, or knock my hand away; she simply slid past me, methodically packing the small blue case which had been in the cupboard.

'There aren't all that many things that fit me as I am now,' was all she said — once, wryly, as though suddenly she felt we were on speaking terms again. But when I said, 'Stay, Liza, and let's see how it works out,' she withdrew again.

I had known her for too long not to realize that she meant what she said. When the case was full, and she was putting her coat on, I picked up the music case that Manton had noticed on his search of the room. Liza had had it for years: it was a cross between a normal music case and a brief case, with a stained old brass lock and a frayed handle. I held it out to her.

'Don't forget this.'

'I won't be needing it,' said Liza.

'You didn't bring anything in it?'

'I didn't even bring it. I left it behind when I first went.'

'But . . . '

Then I recalled that Ingrid had used it.

The key had been in the lock, and she had asked if she might have it, and I had passed it over to her.

'Still mixing us up?' said Liza drily.

I looked at the case I was holding. Where was the key? If it had been among Ingrid's possessions, it was now doubtless in Lake's hands; or Manton's.

Liza sat down on the edge of the bed.

'You're going to open it, aren't you?' she said softly.

'It ought to go to the police,' I said.

'It's probably only got music in it.'

'Yes.'

I got a razor blade and hacked away at the leather round the lock. It was tough going. The skin was scraped away from my fingers. But I succeeded in cutting the stuff away and opening the case.

There were a few sheets of music inside. At the bottom there was a passport, a year out of date, for a Sophie Robinson. The photograph was that of a schoolgirl on the verge of maturity — a young face that yet belonged to an older woman. Although she was very blonde, the features were undoubtedly those of

Ingrid. Inside the passport was an old Control Commission permit for entering and leaving the British Zone of Germany. Sophie Robinson's home address appeared as one of those typically Army combinations of letters and numerals, with only the word 'Holstein' to give any general focus.

I held the stuff out to Liza. She leafed through it.

'Looks as though she went in and out quite a lot,' she observed.

'She never said a word about it to me.'

'School terms,' said Liza abruptly. 'She could have been at school in England, and then gone back to her parents in B.A.O.R., or the Control Commission, or whatever it was.'

I turned the case upside down and shook it out. There were some crumpled pieces of paper — the sort of thing that always accumulates at the bottom of cases like that — and two illustrated leaflets. I picked them up. They were in German, but their meaning was fairly clear. They were handouts for a strip-tease club in Frankfurt. One of the photographs was of

Ingrid, shielded only by a black band from one side of the page to the other, carrying the words 'Ich hab' soviel Talent.'

Liza took them from me.

'Promotion material,' she said. 'I suppose she could always get a job on the strength of these, if all else failed.'

I took the passport and permit back from her. I studied them as though they would tell me all the things I needed to know. The police would certainly be glad of them. This was what they were looking for. They could get busy with a foundation like this, and then the truth would be revealed — and made public.

Ingrid's face, so much younger yet already set in its cool indifference, stared out at me from the passport. Her eyes here were frozen — even less revealing than they had been in life.

Liza said: 'You want to find out for yourself, don't you? Mike, you *need* to find out.'

I was finishing with the band. I had time to spare, time that was going to hang miserably on my hands, and memories that would be choking my mind.

'You've got to go,' said Liza.

'It wouldn't get me anywhere,' I tried. 'I'd sooner stay here — and I'd sooner you stayed. If I go away, you — '

'Mike,' she said, 'I've thought of you every day and every night since I left. It was worst at night. I wondered if you were . . . with her. I wasn't nice and calm and free from jealousy. Don't think that. But I couldn't do battle with Ingrid. She was too fresh, too new. I could only wait. And what I've waited for is still not here. You haven't escaped from her yet, Mike — not by a long way. Maybe you never will. But now you've got to do something about it.'

'The police will make a better job of it.'

'You've got to see it all for yourself,' said Liza. 'Find out what you can. I know in my bones it won't be good. So go; and come back when you're satisfied.'

17

The hospital was a long drive north-west of Hamburg. It stood behind trees in a flat, dark landscape. A lot of building had apparently been done in recent years; this was certainly something more than the hastily constructed Rehabilitation Centre I had been told about.

I swung the car in to the edge of the flinty approach. When I had switched the ignition off I sat for a moment before getting out. I had made no plans. It had been impossible to ask too many questions before starting from England, as I would have aroused suspicion and perhaps brought Lake or Manton on my track. I knew where I was going, but I didn't know what I would do when I got there. It would all be a matter of improvisation. Strictly busking, I said to myself. The situation would shape the questions.

I got out of the car.

There was a flight of steps up to the main entrance. They contrived to look imposing without being in any way noble. I marched up and came into a warm hall. It was too warm; the central heating functioned with excessive enthusiasm.

A man in uniform with epaulettes which made me want to spring to attention emerged from behind a desk in one shadowed corner.

'*Was wunschen Sie?*'

'May I speak to the — er — Medical Records Clerk?'

'*Bitte?*'

I gave him my card. He examined it with polite but aggressive interest.

'English?' he said.

'Yes.'

He indicated a long bench against one wall and walked to it with me. When I was seated he licked his lips and said carefully: 'I will keep you a minute, please.' Then he returned to the bastion of his desk, and made a telephone call. When it was finished he went on sitting there, not passing on any message to me.

I was not kept waiting for long. A

grey-haired man in a lab. coat appeared from one of the corridors which fed into the hall and walked briskly towards me.

'Mr. Merriman?'

I got up and held out my hand. He bowed, and shook it.

'I am Doctor Steig. I speak the English a little. Perhaps I can help you. I will be able to . . . to find you the right person. There is somebody you wish to see?'

The acrid antiseptic hospital smell seeped from the corridors. Somewhere there was the faint sound of trolley wheels along the floor. None of it matched up with the scented, smoky, stale night world in which folk like Ingrid and myself lived. Like Ingrid *had* lived.

I said: 'I'm trying to trace a girl called Sophie Robinson.'

'She has been injured? She is here for an operation?'

'No. Nothing like that. She was here, I believe, just after the end of the war. I'm anxious to find out what happened to her.' It was my first tentative line, this. I wasn't going to admit that I knew what had happened to her: I wanted to know how much I could find out without giving away anything myself.

Steig frowned. He had reason to.

'The end of the war? There was so much here then. So many things. We had many sick from the concentration camps, you know — that was our special task, you know. You are from the Refugee Organization?'

'I'm here privately,' I said. 'I represent no organization.'

He went on frowning. Private individuals were evidently treated warily.

'You are related to the girl?' he ventured.

'In a way, yes,' I said. The next step.

Still he was not happy.

'If there's anybody here who remembers her,' I went on, 'I would greatly appreciate a word with them. I don't want to take up anyone's time too much. It's entirely a personal matter — but one of great importance to myself and . . . and someone else.'

A man crossed the hall, heading for one of the corridors. Doctor Steig watched him absently, then stiffened.

'*Herr Doktor!*'

The man swung round. They exchanged a few words in German, and then the newcomer came towards me.

His hair was almost silver — what there was left of it. He had very blue eyes and a hard mouth. Eyes and mouth were both somehow reassuring; here was a confident, capable man.

'You are asking about Sophie?'

'You knew her?'

'I am Doctor Held.' We went through the usual formalities, Doctor Steig excused himself and went off, and Doctor Held continued: 'I have been here from the beginning. Professor Robinson was a valued colleague. We owe him a great deal.' His English was smooth and effortless, as though he had been used to thinking in the language for a long time. 'You are related to Professor Robinson?'

'Not exactly,' I said. Then I saw that this was not good enough. Doctor Held was, I felt, a man who demanded that everything should be exact. No floundering and blurring here, no pretending that the language difficulty made it impossible to explain precisely what I meant. 'I know people who knew Sophie' — the name sounded unnatural, and I wanted to speak about Ingrid — 'and they are anxious to find out more about her early life.'

'Why? She is in trouble?'

I hesitated. Then I said: 'She died a few weeks ago.'

The stiff mouth slackened. The regret in his face was dispassionate and impersonal. But when he spoke he sounded friendlier.

'So. She was young. It was an accident?'

'Yes,' I said. 'An accident.' I hoped I wouldn't be called on to supply details.

'Come,' he said. 'We will go to my office.'

He led me down a white corridor to a small room containing a cupboard, a desk, three steel and plastic chairs, and a bookshelf with books stacked at surprisingly untidy angles, some reared up in heaps and some actually inserted upside down.

'Please,' he said, nodding towards one of the chairs.

He took a box of cigars from a desk drawer and pushed it towards me. I shook my head. He was silent for a moment, then said:

'Like Professor Robinson and his wife. The child, too — though she was no longer a child, of course.'

I was puzzled. Then I asked: 'Do you mean they died in an accident, too?'

'That is so. When she was seventeen.'

'And after that?'

He looked at me as though I were a patient who refused to disclose important symptoms.

'Is it not for you to speak of that? If you have known her recently, you know what we do not know.'

I took a deep breath. I said: 'Look, Doctor Held, I'd better give you the complete picture. I knew her, but I never discovered anything about her early life. I hoped that one day she would tell me — after we were married.'

'Ah! So. You were to be married.'

'Yes.'

'She did not tell you about her childhood, and now you want to find out.'

'Yes.'

'Will that do you any good?' he asked dispassionately.

'I can't rest,' I said truthfully, 'until I

know who she was. Until . . . until this happened, I didn't even know she had been in Germany.'

'She was German,' said Held.

'With a name like Robinson?'

'She was adopted, and she became a British citizen.' He chose a cigar, cut it, and lit it slowly, peering into the flame. 'I still do not know,' he said, 'if it will help you to learn of her. She had put the past behind her — or shall I say that Professor Robinson insisted on putting it behind her and making her walk away from it?'

'Say what you like, but tell me the whole story.'

'Very well.' Light from the window behind his head gave him a fuzzy silver halo. 'The girl's real name was Sophie Kuhn. Her father was killed on the Eastern Front. Her mother was a doctor, working in an experimental hospital some distance south of here.'

'An experimental hospital?' There had been something about the way he said it.

'That was one description,' said Held. 'It was in fact an establishment where experiments in plastic surgery were carried out. The subjects of the experiments were volunteers; they were given the choice of coming to the hospital from concentration camps, and most of them were glad to come. They were not always glad to stay. A large number of the experiments were not successful.'

'You mean . . . '

'I mean no more than I say,' Held said stiffly. 'The place was investigated by the occupying powers. There were trials and executions. It is over.'

'Is it?' I said, more to myself than to him.

He went on: 'Doctor Kuhn, Sophie's mother, was in charge of the women occupants. She took Sophie round with her wherever she went. The child was ten when the war ended, and for at least two years before that she had been made to watch operations and the results of operations. That was her whole life. The establishment was far from a town, and its staff lived all the time in this self-contained community. Any education Sophie had came from her mother — and it was an unorthodox education! There were not many patients in the hospital when it was taken by the British, and several of those died within a short time. Two women who survived told us about the girl, and how they had pitied her. They described her white face and her staring eyes: they said she looked stunned always.' He stopped. 'You still wish me to go on?'

I couldn't trust myself to speak. I nodded.

'The staff fled, of course. Most of them were quickly rounded up, but Doctor Kuhn and her daughter stayed in hiding for a long time. The doctor had a sister somewhere not far away, and lived in her cottage. They never came out into the open — until one day it must have become too much for Sophie. While her mother was sleeping, the child got out of the house and blundered into some British soldiers. I remember Professor Robinson telling me that he had heard from one of them that even then she had the same cold, stunned expression. She told them where her mother was hiding — and pleaded with them not to say where they had got the information, and not to let her mother see her. Doctor Kuhn was arrested.'

Pity and horror were simultaneous and equal. If Ingrid had only told me . . . Would she, I wondered hopelessly, ever have told me?

I said: 'What happened to her — to the mother?'

'She was tried as a war criminal. And hanged.'

I shivered. 'Sophie . . . ?' It was still the name of a stranger. Sophie equals Ingrid, I tried to say to myself; but this pitiful little German girl was too unreal.

'She was adopted by Professor Robinson and his wife. He was psychological adviser to the local occupation authorities. There was a great deal for him to do in this area. We dealt with people released from various camps, and there were refugees also. From here up through Schleswig-Holstein we had big problems with displaced persons. It is complicated now,' Held added ruefully, 'by refugees from . . . from the other Germany.'

'This Robinson,' I said — 'what made

him choose this particular girl for adoption?'

'He felt that she had to be saved from her memories. She could not simply be dealt with along with others — her upbringing had been too terrible. She could not be integrated in any reformed German society. He was afraid for her, and what had been done to her mind. Perhaps, also, she was a symbol for him — a symbol of all the work he was doing. He insisted from the start that he should adopt her, and he succeeded. It was very difficult. There were so many rules and regulations, and it took him a long time to get permission. But he was a man who would not be deflected from doing what he felt was right. Sophie Kuhn became Sophie Robinson. She was sent to school in England, and spent holidays with them when they went home on leave. Other times she came over here — to this hospital, where Professor Robinson went on working for some time after your authorities had handed it over. It was a different place from the other hospital she had known, but she never looked happy.

Yet she never looked unhappy. It was always the same — that beautiful, set face, and the eyes always watching something none of the rest of us saw.

'We all respected Professor Robinson greatly. We were proud to retain him on our staff. It was a great shock to all of us when he and his wife were killed in an air smash when coming back from leave.

'Sophie came back from school. There was some money left to her in the professor's will, but it was not a great amount. He had been too devoted a man ever to become rich. It would pay for the rest of her schooling, and perhaps help her a little when she started on a career. She was seventeen then. She returned to her school, and during her holidays came here to stay with one of our German doctors and his wife — friends and great admirers of Professor Robinson. Sophie did not complain, but it was felt that she did not like them very much. We were none of us sure what would happen to her when she left school.

'One evening, during a summer holiday, she came in looking frightened. I find that hard to imagine, but I am assured that she looked frightened. She would not say anything, except to deny that there was anything wrong; but next day she had disappeared. Every attempt was made to trace her, but in the Germany of those days it was very easy for anyone who wished to disappear. It is not too difficult even now.'

'And you never heard any more of her?'

Held shook his head. 'Every attempt was made to trace her,' he repeated. 'But we were working hard, and none of us could go all over Germany in search of a girl who had run away from home. It should also be said' — he studied the glowing end of his cigar as ash fell neatly from it into the ashtray — 'that there were some who did not feel about Sophie as the Robinsons had felt. She was so cold and withdrawn that she aroused much resentment. It was said that she did not belong here and we were well rid of her.'

The callousness of it infuriated me. The young girl, frightened by something she could explain to no one, running away and leaving nothing behind her but this sour, inhuman atmosphere . . .

I said: 'I can imagine that she didn't belong here. No doubt she felt it. She probably went to England. Did you check with her school, or any of her friends?'

'The police did that. She did not go to England — or, if she did, it was done very cleverly, and she certainly saw none of her friends.'

She hadn't belonged in England either. There was nothing and no one to whom she could have belonged.

I said: 'What did you think about her — you personally, I mean?'

He hesitated. Smoke wreathed lazily through the bright outline of his head.

'She frightened me,' he said in a low voice, simply.

'Why? A girl of seventeen . . . '

'I saw her often in the year between seventeen and eighteen,' he said, 'when she was staying with my colleague. I never understood her, never got close to her. She was frightening.' Then he put out one hand towards me, apologetically. 'But I am forgetting. You were to marry her. You would have known her when she was grown up and changed. You would have been happy together, I think. And now there is an accident, and it is ended. Forgive me. The person you knew must have been different from the one we knew here — just as she was different from the child who was forced round the experimental hospital by her mother.'

'Different,' I said. 'Yes . . . yes, of course.'

There was an awkward pause. What was there left for me to do but go? I now knew about the young Ingrid, and I was torn by a rage of pity. And it was all too late. Too late to soothe, to mend, to make all things right.

Doctor Held said: 'Is there anything further you wish to know?'

I got up. 'Thank you for telling me what you have done. It was important for me to know.'

'You will stay and have a drink? Perhaps we — '

'Thank you,' I said. 'I must move on. I've got a long journey to make.'

★ ★ ★

Frankfurt next day was hard, harsh and bright. It had a glittering newness that was tough and expensive. There were bars and cabarets everywhere, most of them with American names. Shashlik bubbled in the window of every little cafe. I noticed that a first-rate small American jazz group was playing in the Grosses Haus a few evenings from now. The traffic was murderous: just slowing to look at the poster advertising the concert, I was nearly trapped between a sleek, quiet tram and an aggressive black saloon.

My hotel had a huge counter stretching across the foyer, with enough men behind it to staff a bank. The wall at the back was covered with a dark, ancient tapestry which gave the place an aroma of respectability that even a bank would have envied. I was reluctant to ask where I could find the strip-tease club whose name I had memorized.

There was no need to be diffident. One broad, bald man with a face like von Stroheim and a voice like Noel Coward deferentially gave me full directions. The place had changed its name three times in

261

recent years, but he remembered all its transmutations.

It was some ten or fifteen minutes from the centre of the city, in what looked like a placid little suburb with a typical suburban cinema, one restaurant, and a long road stretching away into the twilight with tramlines narrowing to a point far down it. Entrance to the club involved a membership fee of three marks. After paying this, I edged my way down a narrow staircase into a small cellar.

It was small, but startling in its decor, with a great deal of glass and heavy plush padding all round, as though the owner feared that patrons might fling themselves ecstatically from wall to wall. There was even an infinitesimal balcony. It held four people sitting at a tiny table: they must have wriggled in through a low door, and if they stood up they would certainly bang their heads on the ceiling. A three-piece band was wedged in one corner. The drummer had no room to move his arms, and even the pianist probably had to keep to the middle register of the keyboard if he didn't want to knock a glass over with his elbow.

I had come early. There were three bored-looking men at a table drinking whisky and watching four girls behind the narrow bar. The band played a number, but nobody came on to take any clothes off, and the men did not try to coax any of the girls from behind the bar to dance. It was hard to imagine a place as small as this paying its way — on mere drinks and cabaret alone, that was.

I leaned on the bar. I was served by a girl with black eyebrows pencilled upwards like the spread wings of a seagull. I paid an exorbitant sum for a whisky, and then I said:

'Did you ever have a girl called Sophie in the show here?'

The girl glanced over her shoulder. 'Sophie.'

A blonde with large breasts shuffled along the bar. If she had been any larger, there would have been no room for her to move at all in that confined space.

'*Ja?*'

'I'm looking for a girl — that is, for anyone who knew a girl called Sophie

263

who used to work here.'

'I'm Sophie,' she said in a rich American accent blunted all round the edges. 'You been recommended?'

'I'm afraid you've got it wrong,' I said. 'The girl I'm thinking of is dead. I just wanted to find out if anyone here remembered her.'

Her face, plump and smooth but showing signs of the pudgy whiteness that would get more and more flabby as time went on, sagged into indifference. 'Plenty of girls been here, mister. They come and go. You English?'

'Yes.'

'I thought so,' she said without interest.

'Is the manager here?' I asked.

'He gets here late. Hilde will be here soon. She may know. You can talk to her.'

'Will you tell her I'm here?'

'Sure.'

I sat at one of the tables. Several men drifted in, and a couple of women with them. The girls behind the bar were joined by an older woman with a lean body and a thin, predatory face. She spoke to the one called Sophie and then glanced at me, but did not come across. I kept looking at her, waiting to see if this were Hilde. She made a telephone call on a phone stuck in the corner of a shelf and then went out.

Five minutes later the first part of the show began.

There was very little room for the dancers to move. Three of them came on in single file and writhed to and fro, while the drummer hammered as hard as he could manage on his snare drum rim. One after the other they began peeling sequin-studded garments off. There was a draught along the bar, and the girl nearest to me had goose pimples from her neck down to her knees.

It was soon over, and they ran off to a spattering of applause.

The band played two more numbers, and then another woman came on. It was the older one who had arrived most recently. She was scantily dressed, but she didn't go into a strip-tease. She danced — and it wasn't the sort of dance that would have gone down well at the Tivoli. There was no doubt about her technique:

she was too old for this game, but she made the younger, more attractive girls look like amateurs.

There was a lot of applause for her, but when she came back she had a silk wrap thrown round her shoulders and she didn't cross the floor; she came straight to my table.

'You were asking about Sophie?'

Her American accent was even better than the younger woman's had been. She must have been here when the Americans first arrived in this part of the world.

'I was,' I said, getting up. 'Will you have a drink, while we — '

'There have been many girls called Sophie,' she interrupted curtly. 'Which one are you thinking of — and why do you want to know about her?'

I took the leaflet out of my pocket and showed her the picture.

'That one,' I said.

'Yes, sure,' she said. 'Will you come this way? It'll be easier than in this place.'

The band was starting up a noisy mambo as we left. All their numbers were out of date, but they sounded as exuberant as though the tunes had only just been dreamed up.

We went along a short, narrow passage in which we had to squeeze past two girls wrapped in gauzy veils. There was a small door at the end. The woman opened it and held it open as I edged past her. For a moment I thought I was going to be pushed in and locked in; then she was following me in, closing the door behind her.

The pounding of the bass drum was still loud in here, but there was no other sound from outside. The room held a bed, illuminated by a lamp with a frilly pink shade, and a chair. There were photographs of naked girls — posed in the club — all round the walls.

On the chair sat a hunched woman with an old, twisted face. She wore a cloak over her shoulders, and although I had never seen the face before I knew that this was not the first time I had seen the woman.

She was holding a gun; and it pointed straight at me.

18

'Hilde,' she said to the woman behind me; and then she spoke in German for a moment or two.

The woman called Hilde moved past me and went to stand beside the hunched shape in the chair.

She said: 'It is Sophie Kuhn you ask about?'

'Sophie Robinson,' I said.

The older one laughed. It was a horrible sound. She spoke again, and again Hilde translated for her.

'Why have you come here to make enquiries? Why have you come from England?'

'I knew her there,' I said, 'under another name.'

Hilde translated into German. The woman in the chair leaned forward, peering up at me. Then she nodded and laughed again. And while she was looking, her face upturned, I saw the terrible seams down her cheeks, and the way the skin was puckered and whitened around her eyes. I looked down at the hand holding the gun, and saw that it was a hand I had seen in a photograph — a warped, twisted hand marked with ridges as though huge, clumsy stitches had once been sewn into it.

She spoke, Hilde translated. It made it all unreal and grotesquely formal. There was no point in interrupting or trying to toss questions and answers to and fro. The pace set itself. It was like a game of cards — putting a card down, allowing it to be studied, and then considering the card which the opponent solemnly laid on top of it.

'You are the band leader. She sang with you.'

'That's right. And you're the woman' — I stared past Hilde at the warped creature in the chair, forcing the words out at her although she would have to wait for their translation — 'who persecuted Ingrid . . . Sophie . . . and disfigured her. You arranged for her murder.'

'No,' came the answer. 'The murder was not part of the plan. Not at that time.'

'You hounded her to her death,' I cried. 'You filled her with fear, and made life hell for her.'

The woman smiled. It was a terrifying smile. Its grim satisfaction made me feel weak.

She said: 'I am glad she was afraid. That was what I wanted, more than anything. If I could have kept her afraid for ever, I would not have killed her even in the end. There were times when I wanted to die because of her — because of Sophie Kuhn — and I was not allowed to die. She should not have died if I had had my way.'

'You're mad,' I said. 'What foulness have you got in you? What could she ever have done to you to make you so insane in this . . . this . . . '

I gave up, because there was no description possible.

The woman suddenly reached down for a battered old leather bag on the floor beside her and dropped the gun in it. Her eyes, damp and red-rimmed, met mine,

270

and again she laughed.

She said: 'I am sorry for you. You loved her?'

'Yes,' I said. It was true, wasn't it? It all seemed so long ago, and Ingrid Lee had not been Sophie Kuhn or Sophie Robinson. But I had loved her, hadn't I?

'I am sorry for you,' said the woman again. I watched her as Hilde's American-tinged translation came from beside her, like a loudspeaker placed at an angle. 'If she still means so much to you, I must tell you all I know. Perhaps then you will be able to escape from her and begin to live. But you will not like what I tell you.'

I heard the echo of Liza's voice. *It won't be good.*

I said: 'I know about her wretched childhood. I've already found out about the way her mother dragged her round that hospital and made her watch things she ought never to have seen. If she went wrong afterwards — if she hurt some-body, or got involved in something — I say she needed help rather than hatred. Nothing could justify what you did to her.'

Her laughter was almost hysterical this time. Her voice became guttural with a hatred that, even in a foreign language, blazed out through her words. Hilde's translation was matter-of-fact, but the reality of the hatred was there alongside it.

'That is the story, yes. She was a child sinned against, and a kind English psychologist took her under his wing and tried to give her a normal life. That's the way it goes, huh? But it wasn't like that at all. The child Sophie Kuhn was evil. You do not believe in the evil of a child? To you it's just the way it was for Professor Robinson: a new environment and a few kind words can make the whole thing all right. If there was anything wrong in the first place, it must have been the fault of the mother, or the war, or the world. But I tell you there are some children who are born wicked and will always be wicked. Sophie Kuhn was one. It was not the mother who insisted on taking her round the hospital: the girl herself loved every minute of it. Not all of us realized this. There were some who were sorry for her

— but they were not the ones who had heard her speak. It is a voice I shall never forget. 'Mama, what would happen if . . . ' She would ask that in her hard little voice; and the mother would smile and show her. The mother would bring the instruments and explain to the child just what she wanted to know. And when we screamed, she watched and listened, and when we had stopped she would ask another question. I never saw her smile; but I saw complete happiness in that face of hers, and those watching eyes.

'Few of us survived our experiences in that hospital. When I was younger I was a singer, and I played the piano. I sang in a literary cabaret — and the Nazis did not like that. I stopped, and sang ordinary songs, and played the piano. All I wanted to do was live and be pretty and be happy. But they did not forget. In the second year of the war I was arrested and sent to a camp. Then they moved me on to the experimental hospital. They told me they would carry out experiments which would tell them useful things — all kinds of things to make life better for other people. And they operated on my hands, and grafted skin from my arms to my face, and when I was in the worst pain they asked me — just as an experiment — to see if I could play the piano and sing.

'Sophie Kuhn watched me trying to play the piano. She enjoyed it.

'When the place was liberated there were few left alive. Perhaps only two of those left knew the whole story of Sophie Kuhn — and what happened to the other woman I don't know. I was in bad shape. For months I was insane. I remember none of it. They sent me to a rehabilitation centre — a special wing for those whose minds had cracked . . . had been cracked by evil. It was a long time before I emerged into the world again. And I wanted only one thing. I wanted to find Sophie Kuhn.

'It took me years to find her. The kind men who had wanted to save her and make her happy had done a splendid job. All traces had been covered up. But I was patient. And I had many people working with me. I played a part in a certain international organization which I will not discuss with you, but which gave me contacts all over the country and all over Europe. And one day, visiting one of my agents, I saw Sophie Kuhn. Only now she was called Sophie Robinson. She recognized me, just as I recognized her. And at last there was some expression in her face. Just for a few seconds I saw fear there — and I knew that I wanted to keep that fear there. But she got away from me. She didn't stay around. She disappeared. I had lost her again.'

I began to sense the shape of the rest of the story. Only the details were missing; and now the woman began to supply them.

Sophie had run away to Frankfurt. It was already struggling to its feet again. American forces in the area had plenty of money to spend, and the city itself showed that it had every intention of becoming rich before very long. A beautiful young woman could make more than a comfortable living there.

In due course she arrived at this club — one of the first strip-tease clubs in the city, and one which had survived all the later competition. Here Hilde, instead of merely translating, took over the story herself. She had been the star turn in the place then. She still ran everything here, and she still remembered what Sophie had been like.

'The other girls hated her. It wasn't anything she said or did: it was just the way she was. But we had to keep her on. For the men she was wonderful. Perhaps men like to be sneered at. She was cold and hard, and they went for that. When she stripped she watched them — she loved watching, she got such a kick out of seeing them suffer.'

I remembered Ingrid singing, and remembered how I had felt and how I could sense what the audience felt. And, with a terrible shudder, I remembered her half-veiled eyes, blandly watching me when I made love to her.

'She stayed with us some time.' Hilde glanced around, then swung back as though anxious to hit me hard with the facts, so that I would never forget. 'She spent a lot of time in this room. She made plenty of money.'

'I see.' It sounded lame and ridiculous.

'We had contacts with an organization that she knew nothing about. It was none of her business — and we didn't trust her — but some of the girls . . . '

'Dope!' I said instinctively.

The two women looked at one another. Then the older one shrugged and said something in an undertone.

'It was through this,' said Hilde, 'that Sophie was found again. Found working here.'

The woman — this distorted wreck of a woman who had not given me her name and whose namelessness made her somehow larger than life and somehow more fearsome than death — had once more stumbled across Sophie, and driven her on. Before she could do anything Sophie had disappeared.

The next clue to her whereabouts came in an English newspaper. Plenty of the papers circulated in Germany, and there had been plenty of photographs of the new singing sensation, Ingrid Lee, before this particular one appeared in print; but there was something special about this one. In all the others, Ingrid had been shown as dark. In this one — it was the one taken as I stood beside the car and Ingrid got in — the shadow had cut away her hair, leaving only the oval of her face. She looked as she had looked in her youthful passport photograph. It was this that the woman recognized. It was from this that she took up the trail and came to England in pursuit.

It was an obsession. The remorselessness of it struck a chill to my heart. The thought that, years after the war, anyone could be so set on revenge, was something that I could not grasp. But how many people were there and are there in England who would fail to grasp the vividness of this terror that had once existed?

'I had my contacts,' she said, 'and I used them. I travelled to England, and there I planned to concentrate on the evil being who now called herself Ingrid Lee.'

Her views on why Sophie Robinson had fled to England, and what she did there, would have prodded me into a fury not so long ago. But now the pattern was too convincing. I listened, and even added half-conscious embellishments of my own. The picture was a convincing one: too convincing.

Sophie's passport, renewed just before she disappeared from the family who had taken her over when the Robinsons died, was still just valid. It carried her to England. She did not visit old friends or ask for help from anyone who might have known the Robinsons. Hilde advanced the theory that she had answered a carefully-worded advertisement in a newspaper. There were many such in those days. German girls were invited to work in England, and were met, on their arrival, by men who controlled one of the most flourishing professions in London. Some of the girls were appalled when they found what they had walked into. Many knew before they started out what they were heading for. Sophie could hardly have had any doubts.

'I found out as much as I could,' said the older woman, 'and it looks as though she worked for a man called Shale — among other names. He was arrested only a few months after she arrived, and she and others had to make themselves scarce. She went to ground somewhere, and the next thing was that she was singing with your band.'

'She went to work,' I said, 'in a coffee bar. Then I discovered her.'

And then — we both saw this, and I could not bear the half-amused pity in the woman's dreadful face — the Sophie who had become Ingrid saw what promised to be security ahead of her. I was obviously infatuated with her. She would take me from my wife — coldly, without rushing it, leading me on until I was doing all the pleading — and would marry me, and then she would be comfortable and safe.

That was almost certainly the idea. It fitted so well.

But we were in love. I said it to myself, and tried to say it out loud. But I no longed believed it.

Then that photograph appeared, and the pursuer closed in once more.

From the start Ingrid could have been in no doubt as to who was threatening her. She saw the woman's face in the alley when the bottle of vitriol was poised. There were more telephone calls than she had ever told me about. There was the scalpel thrown at her feet to remind her of the hospital — a scalpel, with its recollections of the past and its intimations of the future.

And there was the ever-present fear that I would find out what she had once been. She had to play down the attacks . . . or blame them on to somebody else.

Which was where Liza proved so useful.

There must have been always a double fear weighing on her — the fear that next time she would be hit harder, and the fear that Liza would suddenly show up and prove that she had not been involved at all. The vicious razor attack showed that the pressure was being stepped up; but still she dared not tell the truth. How close had she been, I wondered, to telling me before she died? She must have known that it could not have gone on much longer.

When Liza did at last show up, Ingrid knew that there was little time left. She had no way of getting in touch with her pursuer directly. But she had a pretty good idea who had been working for the woman in small ways.

Cy Mitchell was a dope addict. He was under the thumb of the man who supplied him — and that man was involved in the organization in which this woman played such a big part. Mitchell was forced to act for them. He was a useful irritant. He could lock a door, slip a photograph into a hotel bedroom . . .

'It was Mitchell, of course,' I said, 'who let you know we were going to The Chord Club that evening when Ingrid was slashed.'

'Of course.'

Ingrid must soon have guessed how Mitchell was implicated. And even before that she had made an enemy of him.

I told of the incident when Mitchell had apparently been ill and Ingrid had given him what we presumed to be some digestive powder. Now it was clear what it had been. Ingrid herself must certainly have known. I recalled now how she had looked at him. She must have found the box and deliberately withheld it from him until he was desperate. She had watched — always the calculating watcher, enjoying herself — and then had seen him almost grovel as she handed over the only thing that could stabilise him.

And Mitchell had understood the look in her eyes.

It was for Mitchell that she sent when Liza telephoned and demanded to see me.

'He told me afterwards,' said the woman, 'that she wanted to get in touch with me. She wanted to know how much I'd take to go away and leave her alone. It was her last chance, and he was the only lead she had. When he said he couldn't do anything right away, and wasn't going to stick his neck out anyway, she began to goad him. He didn't want to argue with the people who supplied him with what he needed. She jeered at him — called him a coward, taunted him because of his drug addiction, offered herself to him and then said she didn't suppose he would know what to do with her. Fear made her more wildly contemptuous than ever. She was hysterical — and she was dealing with an unbalanced man who was only too ready to be hysterical himself. Crazed with dope and the need for dope, unstable . . . He went for her, to shut her up — and strangled her.'

There was something hammering away at my mind. I had wanted to break in, but the formal pattern of her German speech and the following translation made interruption difficult. When she had finished I said:

'Mitchell told you all this — *afterwards*?'

She nodded.

'Before he committed suicide?'

Her voice was calm, and Hilde's voice was calm as she provided the English version. 'He telephoned our contacts and passed on a message to me before he went to see Sophie — Ingrid Lee. I was waiting for him when he got back.'

'You killed him?'

'I understand,' she said, 'that he committed suicide.'

'You're sure it was suicide?'

'He could not have lived. He would have talked.'

'I can talk just as much as Mitchell could have done,' I heard myself saying. It was mad, but I was beyond caring. 'You can't imagine I'll keep my mouth shut about all this? The dope racket . . . if you think I'd go away and say nothing and condone that sort of foulness . . . wrecking people's lives . . .'

She moved in her chair. I half-expected her to get the gun out again.

'Wrecking people's lives?' It was an echo of my own words, resounding through the German and then back again through Hilde. 'Do you know how many lives were wrecked in Europe during the years of the Third Reich? When those years were ended, do you suppose it was easy for the living? Look at me — *look* at me!'

The warped face was thrust at me. The arms rose painfully, and the talons of her hands reached out. I winced involuntarily, and this pleased her.

She went on: 'Drugs saved me. Drugs kept me alive. And when I was conscious once more of being alive, I needed the drugs more than ever to make life tolerable. There are thousands like me. There are men and women everywhere who need to escape.'

'That's no argument,' I said. 'It's . . . it's an evil trade.'

'What do you know of evil?' she demanded. 'What do you know of the darkness? All the world is evil. Any escape from it is justifiable.'

'No,' I said. 'No. This hatred . . . you ought to have learnt to forget.'

I thought she was going to laugh, but the sound died in her throat. 'I do not have long to live,' she said suddenly. 'I am tired. Perhaps you are right. When a lot of us are dead, perhaps things will be better, and you can all be content and forget. Now I have only a few months to live, and I shall do nothing more.'

'If you think you're going to get out of it that way . . . '

'If there is any talk of arresting me,' she said, 'I will kill myself first. Or you, if necessary. I will not go to prison. I have had too much of prison. Now there is only the waiting. It has got worse lately, and it will not last much longer.'

She was not inviting pity. The mere idea of it was monstrous. She was a murderess, a criminal, a wicked creature mixed up in the foulest of all trades. And yet the idea of the law and of punishment seemed equally wrong. Punishment — for this twisted wreck whose suffering had already been so great?

'It will not last much longer,' she repeated. Abruptly her voice was strong again, and Hilde had to translate quickly to keep up with her. 'You must go home, young man. Go back to the safe places where you can talk about learning to forget. There is nothing you can do about this world: it is not yours. Things will go on as they have always gone on. Better go back to your music. Learn to forget, you say. Very well. That is for you to try also: learn to forget.'

I went out through a cluster of girls with plump, soft bodies and hard eyes. That night I did not sleep, and all through the hours of darkness and even the early morning light I saw only the eyes of Ingrid staring at me.

19

I let myself into the flat, and at once knew that Liza was still there. It was a feeling, an awareness, that had nothing to do with the sight, sound or scent of her. I just knew.

I was frightened. Almost I did not want to see her.

I went on in.

Liza was sitting reading. She looked up as I entered the room. I wondered whether she was going to have a boy or a girl — and felt a strange stirring within myself, as though I, too, could sense the child moving.

'Hello, Mike,' she said.

'I . . . didn't expect to find you here,' I said.

She didn't reply.

It ought to have been the most natural thing in the world to cross the room and kiss her lightly on the forehead; and then, if she responded, to kiss her on the mouth. But I could not go towards her. I sat down opposite her. She looked so tranquil.

Then I told her. No polite trivialities, no preamble: I just plunged into the story and told her the lot. When I had finished there was a long silence; and then she said:

'So it was as bad as that.'

She got up, moving heavily but with a grace that was new to me, and poured us both a drink.

'And now what do I do?' I said.

I had no right to ask her for anything. It was not for Liza to advise and guide and organize my life for me. Yet it was automatic: I realized how much I had always depended on her, and how unobtrusively she had always played her part.

'Dave rang while you were away,' she said.

'Oh.' It meant nothing to me.

'Why don't you get in touch with him? Perhaps he'll offer you a job.'

'Dave — offer *me* a job . . . '

She laughed. 'All right, Mr. Merriman.

Perhaps you can work together as equals. That would do both of you a world of good.'

'But — '

'It's only a suggestion,' said Liza quietly. 'You're the one to make the decisions.'

I put my head in my hands. 'I can't go on,' I cried. 'Playing in a band — churning out that sort of music — after being in contact with all this . . . this horror.' Nausea welled up in me. The eyes of Ingrid, and the twisted shape of the tortured woman. The despair and the harshness. The ugliness of the world. 'Nothing can ever be right again. There's no place for trivial things . . . '

'We don't live with horror all the time,' said Liza. 'It's the ordinary things that keep us going, Mike. Maybe we get callous. Maybe we have to, to survive. You'll get used to living again. You will, Mike. Playing in a band is no worse than anything else. A year from now you'll feel as you used to feel — that there's nothing better in the world.'

It was unthinkable. The taste of evil

was still in my mouth.

'Liza, I can't. I'll never be able to — '

'Ring Dave,' she said, 'and talk to him.'

'Right back to the beginning, eh?'

She nodded. 'Back to fundamentals. Work it out from there. You can't carry the troubles of all the wicked world on your shoulders, Mike. Just deal with your own personal troubles.'

I looked at her. 'Those are hefty enough, aren't they?'

'I don't know. That's up to you.'

It wouldn't work, of course. I couldn't dare to hope that it would work. Nothing would ever be right again. Yet I groped desperately.

'You think we could . . . go on? Start again?'

'You've got to start again somewhere,' said Liza, lowering her eyes. 'It's up to you. I can't help feeling that with a family, and a small band — seven-piece, h'm?'

'A seven-piece family?' I laughed wildly, shakily. It was a terrible joke.

'Could be,' said Liza. And it wasn't terrible any longer. 'Seven-piece band, anyway. Think about it, Mike. Let the idea take hold of you — and it'll sort itself out.'

I took a deep breath. I felt weak; and yet I felt all right.

I said: 'And you . . . you're staying?'

She looked up again. 'I think I belong here,' she said quietly.

'You've always belonged here,' I said.

THE END

TURN OF MR. BUDD

Gerald Verner

ernley in Berkshire, Super-
Budd of Scotland Yard is
on holiday at the cottage of
d, Jacob Mutch. However,
ld becomes involved in an
tion. He learns from Jacob's
ur that his cottage has been
— twice. Yet nothing was
Then the man is found in his
brutally murdered. And the
ng day, the body of a known
al is found dead nearby, shot
n the head!

FOREIGN ASSIGNMENT

Sydney J. Bounds

In the unstable Congo region of Africa, the state of Katanga is an oasis of calm. President Tshombe and his government are united; the country's mines and industries supply the West with copper and uranium. But others, who stand to benefit if the government go under, have plans to assassinate the President. Meanwhile, Detective Simon Brand must prevent the assassination and root out the men behind the plot — and he has just seventy-two hours in which to do it . . .

IVE FOR MURDER

ohn Russell Fearn

Mallison was reluctant to
he murdered man's son,
the incriminating evidence
whelming: he'd been alone
father immediately prior to
der and there'd been a bitter
Goldstein was killed trying to
will — unfavourably for his
weapon, a desk paperweight
son's fingerprints, and his
had withdrawn financial sup-
a new West End play in which
was to star. Yet still Mallison
convinced . . .